Praise for the Sudoku Mysteries

Sinister Sudoku

"[A] very entertaining series . . . You do not need to be a fan of sudoku to enjoy the mystery, but if you are, you'll enjoy solving the puzzles and tips scattered throughout the story." —*CA Reviews*

"A wonderful addition to Ms. Morgan's Sudoku Mystery series! The narrative hits the ground running incorporating sudoku strategy with a treasure hunt and a tantalizing whodunit!" —*The Romance Readers Connection*

Murder by Numbers

"A fun read." —*Cozy Library*

"Kaye Morgan has written a cleverly constructed mystery that reflects the finely crafted sudoku puzzles that are included for fans to enjoy." —*The Mystery Gazette*

"Whether you are interested in sudoku or not, this mystery is fun and challenging." —*MyShelf.com*

Death by Sudoku

"The start of a great new amateur sleuth series . . . Kaye Morgan is a talented storyteller who will go far in the mystery genre." —*Futures Mystery Anthology Magazine*

"The characters are likable, the writing fairly smooth, and the plotline reasonable." —*Gumshoe Review*

"Puzzles and codes surround a vast pattern of murder . . . Sudoku lovers (like myself) will be delighted to see on the cover that this is the first of a series." —*Spinoff Reviews*

Killer
Sudoku

Kaye Morgan

BERKLEY PRIME CRIME, NEW YORK

THE BERKLEY PUBLISHING GROUP
Published by the Penguin Group
Penguin Group (USA) Inc.
375 Hudson Street, New York, New York 10014, USA

Penguin Group (Canada), 90 Eglinton Avenue East, Suite 700, Toronto, Ontario M4P 2Y3, Canada
(a division of Pearson Penguin Canada Inc.)
Penguin Books Ltd., 80 Strand, London WC2R 0RL, England
Penguin Group Ireland, 25 St. Stephen's Green, Dublin 2, Ireland (a division of Penguin Books Ltd.)
Penguin Group (Australia), 250 Camberwell Road, Camberwell, Victoria 3124, Australia
(a division of Pearson Australia Group Pty. Ltd.)
Penguin Books India Pvt. Ltd., 11 Community Centre, Panchsheel Park, New Delhi—110 017, India
Penguin Group (NZ), 67 Apollo Drive, Rosedale, North Shore 0632, New Zealand
(a division of Pearson New Zealand Ltd.)
Penguin Books (South Africa) (Pty.) Ltd., 24 Sturdee Avenue, Rosebank, Johannesburg 2196,
South Africa

Penguin Books Ltd., Registered Offices: 80 Strand, London WC2R 0RL, England

This is a work of fiction. Names, characters, places, and incidents either are the product of the author's imagination or are used fictitiously, and any resemblance to actual persons, living or dead, business establishments, events, or locales is entirely coincidental. The publisher does not have any control over and does not assume any responsibility for author or third-party websites or their content.

KILLER SUDOKU

A Berkley Prime Crime Book / published by arrangement with Tekno Books

PRINTING HISTORY
Berkley Prime Crime mass-market edition / July 2009

Copyright © 2009 by Penguin Group (USA) Inc.
Sudoku puzzles by Kaye Morgan.
Cover illustration by Trisha Krause.
Interior text design by Laura K. Corless.

ISBN: 978-0-425-22839-5

BERKLEY® PRIME CRIME
Berkley Prime Crime Books are published by The Berkley Publishing Group,
a division of Penguin Group (USA) Inc.,
375 Hudson Street, New York, New York 10014.
BERKLEY® PRIME CRIME and the PRIME CRIME logo are trademarks of Penguin Group
(USA) Inc.

PRINTED IN THE UNITED STATES OF AMERICA

10   9   8   7   6   5   4   3   2

For my brothers, Charlie and Frank, and my sisters-in-law, Betty and Nancy, for putting up with this author's antics. And to my editor, Michelle Vega, for the same reason . . .

PART ONE:
Standard Sudoku Time

I recently came across a scientific study that claimed the hours between nine and eleven a.m. as the most productive time of day for most people. That led me to wonder—is there an optimal time and place for sudoku?

Certainly, it's best not to tackle a puzzle when you're overtired or distracted—that way leads almost inevitably to disaster. Any other guidelines? Well, personal experience has taught me that taking a break from a solution and returning later allows me to bring new eyes to a puzzle. (Note: this is *not* a good technique for competitive sudoku!)

Even the action of moving from the great indoors to my backyard can free up a logical logjam. So I guess a change of place can help with a puzzle—so long as the new place isn't the bottom of your wastebasket.

—Excerpt from *Sudo-cues* by Liza K

Liza Kelly stood on the balcony of her room, looking down at the water of Upper Newport Bay. It seemed to reflect the almost artificial blue of the California sky overhead.

Sighing in contentment, she turned back to the suite—and had to hide a smile at the sight of her neighbor, Mrs. Halvorsen, through the open door of her bedroom. Mrs. H. stood bent over the queen-sized bed, her hands sunk nearly to the wrists into the mattress on the hotel bed.

"It seems awfully . . . mooshy." The older woman's plump cheeks creased in a dubious frown.

Of course, for Mrs. H. and her generation, the only healthy mattress was a rock-hard super-firm.

"It's a pillow-top mattress," Liza explained. "Trust me, it's expensive enough to go along with a suite like this."

In what Liza liked to consider her "old career"—partner in a major Hollywood publicity firm—she had booked suites like this in even fancier places than the Rancho Pacificano resort for the rich, the famous, and sometimes even the talented.

Her new career as sudoku expert had involved considerable travel recently, publicizing her newly syndicated newspaper column. Since Liza was mainly traveling on her own dime, the accommodations had been more Comfort Inn level than deluxe resort.

But the invitation for the West Coast Sudoku Summit allowed her to publicize the column in style. It wasn't just that there was a five-figure prize for coming in first at the tournament, or that there would be national news coverage. Her friend Will Singleton had offered an all-expenses-paid trip for two from Liza's hometown of Maiden's Bay, Oregon, to one of the swankiest joints on the coast of beautiful Orange County, California.

That "for two" part had thrown a major curve into Liza's planning for the long weekend. If her career was hectic, her personal life had stepped well over the line into just plain crazy. She had way too many candidates for the post of California companion.

First, there was her husband, Michael Langley. Well, ex-husband. Or was there such as thing as almost-ex-husband? His storming out of her life a year and a half ago had prompted some heavy soul-searching on Liza's part. She'd gone on to return to Maiden's Bay and establish what became the basis of her new life. The closer they came to the paperwork that would finally end everything, however, the more reluctant Michael became at calling it quits on their marriage. To tell the truth, Liza felt the same reluctance.

The only thing that kept them both from a stereotypical romantic happy ending was Kevin Shepard. Liza had bumped into her old high school boyfriend, newly single, when she returned to Maiden's Bay. Now the manager of a boutique country inn, Kevin had definitely expressed interest in her, much to Michael's annoyance.

And then there was Ted Everard, state police sergeant. He and Liza had started out as investigative rivals when Liza got involved in yet another murder. But they had moved on to friendship—and something warmer—by the end of the case. Partly, Liza had to admit, that was because

Ted's behavior had looked so much more adult compared to what Michael and Kevin were demonstrating at that time. The guys had been carrying on like characters from a bad teen comedy.

Part of the problem with being an adult, however, was that Ted's job kept him traveling the length and breadth of Oregon, chasing crime statistics. Even though he enjoyed sudoku puzzles, Ted couldn't free up his schedule for the Sudoku Summit. And Liza by no means wanted to encourage her other suitors.

So the men in her life weren't on the invite list.

That left Mrs. H.

Besides, Mrs. H. definitely could use a break. Liza had always thought of her next-door neighbor as grandmotherly, but lately Elise Halvorsen was definitely looking her age. Money worries and a traumatic loss in the family had carved deep lines in her cherubic face. Liza had been able to help with those problems, but she thought it would be nice for Mrs. H. to relax in the California sun. And she'd definitely make for a quieter and more restful suitemate than any of the other choices.

Peace and quiet, Liza had found, were good things to enjoy before competitive sudoku. They were also good in general. That's why Liza had turned off her cell phone while standing in line at the Portland Airport and hadn't turned it on since.

She smiled now as Mrs. H. took off the lightweight straw hat whose wide brim fluttered like wings with every move she made. Another sign of the difference in generations— Mrs. H. had donned her Sunday best for the plane trip. Liza, in contrast, wore a pair of sloppy jeans and a denim jacket, both well worn and comfortably worn in. She'd packed a couple of nicer outfits into a carry-on bag, while Mrs. H. had seemingly poured half her house into a pair of large suitcases.

Mrs. Halvorsen took off her hat and skimmed it through the air to land on the bed. "I think I'll follow your example and get into something looser," she said. "Then I think I'll find someplace where I can sit in the sun."

"I'll be doing the opposite and changing into something less comfortable," Liza sighed. "Will has a media event with the major players at the tournament." Shrugging, she patted the bulge of her cell phone in her shoulder bag. "At least I haven't had a deedle on my phone."

Mrs. H. gave her a look. "Is 'deedle' even a word?"

"As much a word as 'mooshy,'" Liza replied. "It's the sound my phone makes when—"

The suite's telephone began to bleat.

"When it rings." Liza glanced at her watch. "Maybe it's Will checking in early."

She picked up the phone. "Thank God I got you!" Ava Barnes exclaimed in her ear. "We had a major technical meltdown at the office—"

The office in question was the satellite office of the *Oregon Daily*, where Ava was managing editor, managing, in part, Liza's new career as a nationally syndicated columnist.

"And we lost some stuff, including your cushion," Ava went on.

That cushion didn't offer much in the way of comfort to anyone but Ava—it represented finished articles for Liza's column, ready in advance. Well, it could lead to some *discomfort* for Liza. "Lost?" she echoed, "as in—"

"Not able to be retrieved by available technology," Ava finished. "I'm afraid we'll have to get your backup copies . . ." Her voice died away for a moment. "You do have backup copies at home, don't you?"

"Ye-ess." Liza held on to the word a little longer than necessary. Yes, there should be copies in her home office computer—a rather grand term for a clunker PC with an obsolete operating system precariously balanced on an old table in the corner of the living room. "They may be a little difficult to locate." Liza didn't keep the most orderly hard drive. For that matter, after her frantic last-minute packing had strewn stuff around, the living room looked as if a squall line had passed through.

Was there even an underwear-clear path to the computer?

At least Rusty wouldn't be rooting around in the mess. Liza's setter-mix was in a fancy kennel, hopefully enjoying the doggie equivalent of a resort weekend.

Liza sighed. "Well, you've got the key. Just be aware that the place is still—um—"

"A disaster?" Ava laughed. "I was in your bedroom when you were just fifteen. I remember!"

Yeah, but that was when Mom was still around, making sure I cleaned up every once in a while, Liza thought, but she didn't say it.

"Or you could do a quick piece on this tournament and e-mail it in," Ava suggested.

That got another sigh from Liza. "Will Singleton specifically asked me to hold off on any columns during the tournament," she said. "Part of his whole sponsorship agreement involves media rights."

Ava's voice soured a bit. "So we'll just have to rely on what you've already written—wherever you've hidden it."

On that happy note they hung up. Liza turned to Mrs. Halvorsen. "I'm sor—"

The phone rang again.

"I guess Ava has something else—" Liza apologized as she brought the receiver up.

"Surprise!" Kevin Shepard's voice boomed out, apparently loud enough for Mrs. H. to hear on the other side of the room.

"Is that Kevin?" she asked.

"I'll tell you in a second," Liza told her, "right after I switch to an ear that still works."

She shifted the phone to hear Kevin still burbling away. "We've met at trade shows and even appeared on a panel together, so even though the place is jam-filled for your tournament, Fergus found a room for me." Kevin paused for a second. "I guess it's staff quarters—I've got a view of the manure pile behind the stables."

"Room?" Liza found herself struggling to keep up with Kevin. "You mean you have a room? Here?"

"Isn't it great?" Kevin asked. "It wasn't a sure thing, so I didn't want to say anything. But Fergus came through, so Jimmy Perrine flew me down in his plane."

Liza knew Jimmy Perrine. He wouldn't mind flying down from Oregon, so long as his passenger filled the tanks on his plane. Given the price of aviation fuel, Kevin had paid a pretty penny for his surprise.

Well, he was still too excited to notice that Liza was more aggravated than amazed. Silently sighing, she tried not to pour too much cold water all over him.

"As surprises go, it beats finding a dead body," Liza told him. "You know, though, this isn't a vacation for me. This is a tournament. I'm here working for the weekend."

"I figured I could cheer you on," Kevin replied.

"Not too loud," Liza warned him. "They don't have much in the way of space for an audience, and the rules are pretty tough."

"Can you spend some time now?"

"Mrs. H. and I just arrived," Liza said, "and I have some sort of media thing to do. Can I get in touch with you later?"

"Try me on my cell," Kevin advised her. "I don't think there's a landline in here."

Liza cut the connection and looked helplessly at Mrs. H. Her hand was still on the phone when it rang again.

"Liza?" There was no mistaking the voice on the other end—Michael Langley, Liza's on-again, off-again husband. "Thought I'd check to see if you'd gotten in."

"Just about," Liza said. "I thought you were all wrapped up with that new script you're working on—what was it?"

"The Surreal Killer." Michael coughed. "I'm afraid

production is going to be held up for a while—twenty-eight days, at least."

As an insider in the Business—the film business, what other business would be capitalized in the home of Hollywood—Liza caught the implication immediately. Twenty-eight days was the standard length for a rehab stint.

"So, since I'm at a bit of a loose end here . . ." Michael began.

"Michael, you'll be going almost completely through L.A. to get down here," Liza said, shooting a horrified glance at Mrs. H.

"I thought about that." Michael sounded hugely pleased with himself. "That's why I'm already here."

"You booked into the resort?" Liza asked as her neighbor flumped down into the mooshy bed.

"Do I look like I'm made of money?" Michael replied.

Liza knew exactly how much his freelance writing and script doctoring had brought in. Financials were the first part of their almost-divorce process.

"I found a room not too far away," Michael said.

"Where? Huntington Beach, Costa Mesa?"

"Anaheim," Michael admitted.

Liza firmly forced herself not to giggle. Anaheim—home of Disneyland. "Look, I've got to get Mrs. H. squared away, and then there's a publicity thing. Can I call you later?"

"Use my cell," Michael said. "I think I'll be roaming for a while. There are about a million kids here, and none of them are using their inside voices."

As if on cue, a muffled, high-pitched shriek came over the phone.

Liza forced back that laugh again. "So I hear."

Michael signed off, and Liza prepared to apologize to her neighbor yet again—except the damned phone rang.

It took everything she had not to scream "WHAT?" into the receiver.

"Liza?" Another familiar voice spoke into the silence. "Ysabel Fuentes here."

"Ysabel?" The good news was that Markson Associates would be working at top efficiency. Ysabel was the mainstay of the office, except when she quit over arguments with the boss—and Liza's partner—Michelle Markson.

The bad news—"Hold for Michelle."

"Liza, dear." Michelle came on before Liza could say anything. "You really have to be more responsible with your cell. Ysabel wasted considerable time trying to get in touch with you—"

Five minutes, at least.

"You have a client arriving at the Anaheim Airport approximately twenty minutes from now." Considering her choice of pronouns, Michelle was definitely dropping this in Liza's lap.

"Gemma Vereker just landed on a flight from New York. Turns out she signed up for this tournament of yours under the name 'Tanya Brand.'"

That was the name of the cool-girl teenager Gemma had played years ago on *Malibu High*. Back home in Maiden's Bay, Liza had tried in vain to reproduce the character's hairstyle. Unfortunately, she didn't have a hairdresser available on set to move in between every scene.

"Anyway, I arranged for a helicopter to move Gemma from LAX to John Wayne Airport. Ridiculously childish name for a place where people have to do business," Michelle sniffed.

Then her voice took on a tinge of malicious glee. "And I charged it to Gemma's manager, the despicable Artie Kahn. This is just a quick heads-up so you can arrange ground transportation and, of course, handle client relations for the weekend—make sure she has pencils for the puzzles or whatever."

With that, Michelle rang off and Liza frantically phoned the front desk to track down Will Singleton. She still had to get out of her traveling clothes and into something presentable, but she figured the driving spirit behind the West

Coast Sudoku Summit would definitely be interested in having a movie star at his publicity to-do.

As for the rest?

Liza sighed again, even more deeply.

Good-bye quiet weekend, Liza silently lamented. *Hello calamity.*

2

Will nearly jumped through the phone when Liza called about Gemma Vereker. He had a car on the way to the airport before Liza got into the shower.

Now she strode down the hallway to the Hebrides Room, where Will had told her the pretournament publicity fest was scheduled. She was showered, spiffed . . . and somewhat puzzled.

Why would a resort with a pseudo-Spanish name and architecture on the outside have a Scottish name on the inside? she wondered.

Maybe she could ask Will Singleton. Liza stepped through the big double doors and glanced around the reception room. There was a good crowd inside, mostly media types judging from the amount of canapés being eaten. Like a Napoleonic army, newspeople tended to travel on their stomachs.

It took her a moment to pick out Will Singleton. He was shorter than most of the people milling around, so they tended to hide him from sight.

Liza grinned as she made her way toward him. Short and slight, Will always reminded Liza of Jiminy Cricket.

During the past year, however, he'd grown a salt-and-pepper beard—more salt than pepper, really. Now it made him look more like Papa Smurf, except Will didn't have that blue complexion.

Will stood by a podium set up on the opposite wall from the entrance. Just as she got to him, his cell phone began to bleat. He put up a hand, then began digging for his phone, almost losing the portfolio he was carrying tucked under his arm.

Liza reached out to take it, but Will shook his head. "There are things in here the competitors aren't supposed to see."

Well, thanks, big guy. Liza shot him a measured look as Will stuck the portfolio on the podium, making sure its strap was fastened, then opened his phone.

"Singleton here." Will listened for a moment, his face brightening. "So we're set?" Then he sighed. "Of course, why should this be different from anything else today? So you're waiting in the lobby? Call me again when you're set."

Will closed the phone and gave Liza his attention. Even then he couldn't hide the stress in his face. "Ms. Vereker is in the building, but she wants a shower before facing the public." Will kept his voice low but he was just about rubbing his hands together in anticipation. "Would you mind keeping this under your hat for a bit? I haven't mentioned this to our sponsor yet."

He broke off, glancing over Liza's shoulder. "And speaking of sponsors," he said a bit more loudly, "here's someone I need to introduce to you. Liza Kelly, this is Charlotte Ormond of Satellite International News Network."

"Call me Charley," the petite redhead said. She had the determinedly perky features of a professional cheerleader—or a TV news reporter.

"I'm sure you've heard how sponsorship from the network allowed us to expand this year's tournament," Will went on. "Charley is coordinating the on-air coverage."

Liza nodded. As at least a part-time publicity person, she'd followed the start-up of SINN with interest. The network was the brainchild of Ward Dexter, yet another Australian media mogul trying to conquer the American market. Like Rupert Murdoch, he'd established a foothold by purchasing some near-defunct newspapers, including the *Seattle Prospect*.

The next move in the playbook was to capture some American TV screens, but Dexter had been outmaneuvered in his attempts to acquire some broadcast or even cable holdings. So he'd gone out of the box—way up high, into orbit, in fact.

Truth be told, though, the new network's content remained remarkably earthbound—conservative political commentary leavened with a flashy mélange of celebrity news and risqué scandal. As Michelle Markson had mentioned, "SINN certainly lives up to its name."

"I don't know how our staid sudoku fest will come across on SINN," Liza told the newswoman. "You might have the same problem Fox did covering the NHL."

"We're hoping for something more like the World Poker Tournament," Charley admitted with a gleaming grin, "alternating shots of the puzzles with commentary from Will as the creator and real-time coverage of selected competitors working on the solutions."

Liza glanced at Will, and then at the camera crew that caught up to Charley. "You're going to have a bunch of these guys looking over our shoulders while we work?"

"It was in the application form," Will said defensively.

Liza knew she should have looked over that collection of legal gobbledegook more carefully.

"Our zoom technology will keep it from getting obtrusive." Charley's assurance sounded well rehearsed. "One of the reasons we're here is that the grand ballroom is surrounded on four sides by a raised gallery. We'll have most of the cameras up there."

"Have you had much experience with sudoku?" Liza

tried to keep the dubious tone from her voice as she asked the question.

"I covered the big fuss in Australia last year where sudoku stopped the trial," Charley said.

Liza nodded, knowing the story. Australian jurors were given notebooks to record important points or testimony. In the middle of a major trial, somebody noticed jurors were making notes vertically instead of horizontally. It turned out they were actually playing sudoku instead of listening and a mistrial was declared, at the cost of about a million Australian dollars.

"That was probably the biggest sudoku story to date," Charley said, "at least, until now. We're going from Mistrial Sudoku to . . . Killer Sudoku."

"The name's taken." Liza stopped as the looks on both Will's and Charley's faces told her that point had been discussed before. No need to explain that killer sudoku was a variant where, in addition to the usual sudoku rules, solvers had to fill in random-shaped "cages" with digits that would add up to a specified total.

"Yes, your base audience might know that, but our audience won't. I've got our lawyers looking into whether it's been copyrighted," Charley murmured, and this time Liza sent Will a more charitable look. As many in the forefront of a trend discover the hard way, the suits—and even a perky, petite suit like Charley Ormond—are more concerned with audience expansion, control . . . and branding.

If you don't watch out, Will, this could end up as Killer SINN-doku, Liza silently warned as Will and Charley walked off, the camera crew trailing behind.

"Will must be commended for bringing sudoku to a wider public," a voice at Liza's elbow said. "Too bad he had to turn into a media whore to do it."

Liza bit back a retort when she saw who it was. If Will Singleton was the Father of American Sudoku, Ian Quirk was the Wicked Stepbrother. She'd run into him at sudoku conferences over the years. Ian had a devious genius at creating puzzles. And his grasp of the issues behind the puzzles impressed even academic audiences.

The rules of sudoku were simple. Take a square grid with eighty-one spaces, spread twenty to thirty clues around, and fill in the empty spaces with the digits 1 to 9 without repeating them in any of the puzzle's nine rows or columns. To kick it up a bit, the puzzle is also divided into nine three-by-three subgrids, sets of nine spaces that also must be filled with the magic digits . . . again with no repetitions.

Millions of sudoku lovers around the world tackled the challenge. They didn't have to crunch numbers, just use logic to place the right digits in the right places. Introductions to sudoku always stressed the fact that no arithmetic was required, but the theory underpinning the puzzles depended on the kind of math that filled blackboards in places like M.I.T.

Ian Quirk was a guy who massaged numbers for a living—his civilian job was with a Las Vegas odds maker. And his devious streak didn't just stop at creating puzzles.

"So what brings you out of the desert, Ian?" Liza asked.

Quirk smiled, a brief twitch on his sharp, intense features. "A tournament with the backing to offer a generous prize," he replied, "not like those penny-ante contests the newspapers come up with."

"I thought you'd given up on tournaments," Liza said in surprise. And vice versa. Ian Quirk had a reputation somewhere between John McEnroe and Bobby Fisher. His complaints and demands on matters like heating, lighting, noise, allergens, and seat position had become the stuff of legend—and not in a good way.

"You didn't want tournament staff within twenty feet of you—but TV cameramen are okay?"

Quirk gave her a smile with all the genuine emotion of a casino croupier. "We all have to make sacrifices to expand the audience—and win a fat purse on TV."

And he calls Will a media whore, Liza thought.

"You were the only sudoku name at last year's tournament." Quirk suddenly changed the subject.

"I don't know that I'd call myself a sudoku name," Liza said, "but Will did ask me to come."

"The prize then was basically a plastic trophy," Quirk went on. "And that actor won it—the one who later got killed."

My friend, Liza thought, *not that it seems to mean much to you.* She let the silence between them stretch.

He finally realized she wasn't taking his bait and spoke up.

"This year I've seen more sudoku types attending." He suddenly turned, extending a hand. "Do you know Barbara Basset—of the Sonoma Beach Bassets?"

"Call me Babs." The blond woman was maybe a few years older than Liza, but she had the same petite, near-anorexic figure as Charley Ormond—and the manner of Queen Elizabeth. If anything, she was more consescending. "And you are?"

"Liza Kelly." Liza kept her best publicity agent mask in place as she shook hands. She'd never met Babs Basset, but she'd heard of her—generally horror stories from sudoku fans in the Greater San Francisco area. If Babs fell off the Golden Gate Bridge, that end of Sudoku Nation would pray for the sharks.

Birds of a feather, Liza thought, looking at the two. *Or maybe snakes of a scale might be a better description. I expect Will knows what he's getting into. He's a big boy, after all.*

Babs gave her a well-practiced smile. "You've got that sudoku column the *Chronicle* picked up." Liza had nothing to complain about in the words, but Babs's tone made the venture sound like the quaintest, most amateur thing imaginable.

"Yes," Liza said. She didn't add anything to the statement. Why give Babs a handle to belittle her?

"I'm staking out a presence in new media," Babs went on. The implication that Liza's column was hopelessly old media dropped with all the subtlety of a meteor impact. "The website is set up, and we're looking to cement a network connection." Babs's eyes strayed to Charley Ormond and her camera crew. "I certainly wish you every success—"

"LIES!" a deep voice thundered out.

For a second, Babs lost her façade of hauteur.

But no, it wasn't someone calling Babs on her flow of insincere good wishes. It was just that Scottie Terhune tended to shorten everyone's name to just one syllable. Beefy arms surrounded Liza in a bear hug. "How ya doin', Lize?" he said, still holding on to her like a cute prize he'd won at a circus sideshow.

Scottie finally let her loose with an irrepressible grin. "I see you hooked up with IQ and BB," he said, again displaying his reductive genius with names.

Babs Basset recoiled as if she were afraid Scottie would soil the hem of her dress. Ian was already striding away.

Scottie's grin just got bigger. "Sweethearts, the two of them." He barely bothered to moderate his booming voice. "Sorry I missed you last year, but I had a conflict—a *Trek* convention down in San Diego."

Liza laughed out loud, fingering the woefully inadequate *Trek* uniform top stretched across Scottie's chunky torso. "Aren't you tempting fate, wearing this? I thought *Trek* guys in red shirts were the first to get eliminated."

"That's Classic *Trek*, and this is a *New Generation* costume. Besides, it's my lucky shirt. I won my first sudoku tournament wearing this."

Liza didn't suggest that Scottie's victory must have been some years and several sizes ago.

Scottie must have seen something in her eyes, though, because he said, "I wouldn't go talking trash about eliminations, Lize. This time around, you've got some serious competition. Believe it or not, there's a Vegas betting line on this hoedown. The favorite is Ian Quirk."

"Sentiment for the local boy?" Liza asked.

Scottie shook his head. "Those guys would run down their own mothers rather than give them even odds. Your new best friend Babs is rated to come in fourth."

His grin returned. "They've got me for second."

Liza laughed and shrugged. "Does that make me number three?"

"Try again!" Scottie held up one hand with all fingers outstretched. "You're number five. Looks like the boys in Vegas don't like your touchy-feely articles. They don't think you have the killer instinct to come out on top."

He turned, snagging the arm of a passing figure. "Here's number three."

Even with the kidding and horseplay, Liza couldn't repress a spurt of annoyance. The Vegas mavens thought that Roy Conklin was more of a competitor than she was?

Liza watched Roy trying to shake Scottie loose. "Leggo, Terhune." The guy was just a tad younger than Liza, but an adolescent whine crept into his voice.

Admittedly, he looked much younger, with a round face and a snub nose—and an expression that looked as if he'd just had his hair ruffled and been given a wedgie.

He might be teaching high-order math up in Seattle, Liza thought, *but Roy still has flashbacks to the days when he was a nerd.*

"Maybe we'd better get this show on the road before you start a riot," Liza told Scottie.

He backed off, looking abashed. "Sorry, man."

Liza spotted Will off in a corner, listening on his cell phone. He was just about glowing with anticipation as he clicked the phone shut and headed for a podium in the front of the room.

He settled behind it, and a silence fell on the crowd.

"Thank you, everyone, for attending our tournament kickoff here at the splendid Rancho Pacificano," Will said. "Even more to the point, thank you to our generous sponsors."

Liza noticed that Charley Ormond was too busy to acknowledge the props, directing her camera crew.

"I'd also like to thank our host. Let's have a few words from Mr. Fergus Fleming." Will's phone began to ring. "And not a moment too soon."

Fergus—wasn't that the name Kevin mentioned when he talked about pulling strings to get into the resort?

A tall man with a head of flaming red hair and a beard to match came over to loom beside Will. As Fergus Fleming bent forward to the microphone, Liza could see that even though his suit was expensively and conservatively cut, it certainly didn't hide his wide shoulders.

"Thank you, Will, and let me say it's a pleasure to welcome all of you."

For some reason, that seemed to provoke a fit of coughing from Babs Basset, who had moved front and center before the podium.

Glancing at her, Fleming checked his smooth flow of words, his voice taking on more of a Celtic burr. "As managing partner, I've tried to make Rancho Pacificano a premier modern lifestyle destination."

Well, that explains the Spanish-Scottish combination, Liza thought.

"For all of those staying here, our amenities are at your service. For those of you who aren't, well, you can see all you're missing."

That got a laugh from the assembled guests.

"And for the contestants in this tournament, the best of luck to you!" Fleming waved as some flash cameras went off. Then he stepped over to shake hands with Will, who had to jam his phone into a jacket pocket. More camera flashes and jockeying from the video crews.

Liza just happened to spot a blond head moving from behind the podium—where Will had left his portfolio.

Well, maybe the contents weren't for competitors' eyes. But unless Babs had a photographic memory, even if there were originals of tournament sudoku in there, she couldn't hope to memorize them.

Will moved back to the podium. "In a moment I'll introduce some of the sudoku experts who have come from several nearby states and cities to participate in this year's tournament," he said. "But first I have a surprise announcement. Could I direct your attention to the main entrance, please?"

Charley Ormond was glaring daggers at Will for departing from the agreed-upon script, but she turned her camera crew around.

"It turns out we have a sudoku fan who registered under an alias for reasons of privacy," Will said. "Now, though, she has graciously agreed to let me introduce her, although she really needs no introduction. Ladies and gentlemen, Ms. Gemma Vereker."

3

The double doors in the rear of the room opened, and Gemma Vereker strode into the room. She couldn't have looked more like a movie star if she'd made her entrance trailing a mink coat behind her.

What Liza really found impressive was that Gemma did the job strictly on presence rather than props. Gemma's suit was stylish but understated, and the star's hair was shorter and more silvery than Liza remembered from recent pictures.

Well, Gemma always had a reputation for being smart. Maybe she's reinventing herself—and I wonder if she had some advice on that from Michelle.

The newspeople immediately began peppering the star with questions, but Gemma struck the perfect tone. "I've enjoyed sudoku puzzles for some years now—they've helped pass a lot of time on film sets. And when I heard of a tournament only a short distance from Hollywood . . . well, I had to give it a try."

She gave the photographers a dazzling smile. "But I'm hardly a star at sudoku, so I hope you'll give your attention to the serious competitors at this tournament."

As Will introduced the sudoku pros, Liza kept her publicist's smile in place and glanced around. Even laid-back Scottie and shy Roy looked less than overjoyed at Gemma's surprise appearance.

Sharing the spotlight with a genuine A-list celebrity definitely cuts into their fifteen minutes of fame—more like fifteen seconds these days, Liza thought. *The press, not to mention the paparazzi, will be glued to her from here on out.*

Fergus Fleming joined Gemma and Will at the podium. "And now—a toast to success!"

Uniformed waiters began circulating through the room, carrying trays of long-stemmed glasses.

"Champagne, ma'am?" a voice at Liza's elbow asked.

"I don't know if it's a good idea before a competition," Liza began, then broke off as she gawked at the familiar face above the uniform jacket.

"Kevin! You're not supposed to be here!" she hissed.

"Well, I don't have a formal invite, that's true." Kevin's tanned face cracked into a smile. "But Fergus is a little shorthanded, and I thought this was a way I could earn my room . . . not to mention catching a few minutes with you."

He raised the tray again. "Shall we drink to it?"

Liza took a glass for the toast but then returned it. "Not too long after this, I'll have to tackle the first round of competition. I don't think a drink is the right preparation."

Or having people springing idiot surprises on me, she could have added but didn't.

They didn't have time for any more conversation. Gemma Vereker swept up to them both, placing an empty champagne flute on Kevin's tray while picking up a replacement.

"I'm really sorry to drop out of the sky on you like this," Gemma apologized to Liza. "When I decided to come out here, I did try to talk to you about it, but apparently you aren't in the office much. And Michelle did say it was okay."

They exchanged a look over that, sharing the unspoken Hollywood knowledge—anything Michelle Markson says, goes.

"I hope you didn't mind that bit of theater from Will Singleton," Liza replied.

Gemma laughed. "He seems a nice enough man, and as theater goes, it was fairly benign. Lord knows, I've added a bit of star power to much loonier causes."

"Liza, dear." Babs Basset deftly shouldered her way past Kevin like a linebacker while still looking perfectly ladylike. It appeared she had gifts Liza had never suspected. "Would you mind introducing us?"

Glancing around, Liza saw that all her sudoku rivals were bearing down on Gemma, to the accompaniment of camera flashes and several advancing video cameras.

Liza hoped her smile didn't look as cynical as she felt. This had nothing to do with sudoku solidarity or even celebrity per se. What Babs and the others were angling for was a photo opportunity. Planting themselves beside a famous face enhanced their chances of appearing on a newscast or in a newspaper photo.

It meant less to Liza. Her job had left her with a huge collection of photos of herself accompanying the famous, the infamous, and everything in between.

Michelle's array of "star-effer pictures," as she called them, was even larger. She always threatened to use them to decorate the office powder rooms and bring some of the clients down to earth.

Again, Gemma played her role flawlessly, greeting her prospective opponents as if they were old friends. She even patted Roy Conklin on the cheek. "With a face like that, you could have made a fortune as a child star," Gemma said.

Roy turned bright red and began stammering a response. Gemma leaned toward him. "That's not necessarily a good thing, though. You don't want to be treated like a kid forever."

For just a second, Gemma's face hardened in a sharp frown. Then, just as quickly it was gone as the star bantered with Roy about his academic career. "Sounds a lot more grown-up than my career in make-believe."

Liza's antennas were out and quivering, though. Even a momentary lapse like that from a star was reason for a publicist's concern. She remembered a publicity disaster from way before she even thought of getting into the business.

A seventeen-year-old Gemma Vereker (or Gem Verrick, as she was known then) wanted more time off to prepare for her college boards. Her parents, who were managing her career, wanted her to stick with *Malibu High* for as long as the show stayed on the air. Some of the longer-running characters were in their midtwenties.

This artistic disagreement wound up in a very public court case as Gemma had herself declared an emancipated minor—and discovered that her folks had turned all her earnings into a fancy house, fancy cars, fancy clothes, and a fancy lifestyle for themselves. They literally didn't have enough money left in the bank, despite the millions she'd earned, to pay for her college education.

Gemma often talked about how a couple of small movie parts and a waitressing career had gotten her through college. But Liza had noticed her client never, ever mentioned her parents.

A curious crowd continued to swirl around them even as the sudoku contingent left. Gemma had some practical questions to ask about the tournament. Then Liza caught someone saying, "'Scuse me. Pardon me," and turned to see another familiar figure making his way through the onlookers.

Liza's eyebrows rose. *Speak of the devil. I think of Gemma's old managers, and here comes her present one.*

Michelle Markson didn't have a good word to say about most of her clients' business managers. It was just that Artie Kahn was an especially juicy target. For one thing, he looked like a stereotype—medium height, a shade past medium weight, a bit of a nebbish except for his clunky square glasses and the world's worst hairpiece. The toupee had to be expensive; it perfectly matched what remained of Artie's graying mouse-colored hair. But Artie's toupee made that construction on top of Donald Trump's head look not only natural, but attractive.

If anything, Artie looked a little worse for wear today. His Zegna suit was rumpled from sitting in Friday traffic from Century City to Newport Beach. Even his hairpiece seemed slightly askew.

He edged up to Gemma. "Darling, I didn't even know you were in town until I got that call about the helicopter. Welcome back from New York."

The way he leaned forward made him almost look fawning. Gemma, however, stepped aside. "If you found out I'm here, no doubt you know I'm staying for the tournament. Just for this weekend, I'm going to enjoy myself. We can discuss business on Monday."

Artie took that for the dismissal it was. "Sure, Gemma, sure," he said, backing away.

Liza watched him leave. *I never knew that Gemma shared Michelle's take on Artie.*

Before Artie was out the door, Fergus Fleming arrived at Gemma's side, shaking hands and introducing himself. Yes, photo flashes went off in the background, but Liza saw something of Kevin in the big Scotsman—he was being every inch the hotelier.

Gemma took his arm. "I was quite pleased to see that there were no plants in my room. I know luxe places like this like to decorate with them. For me, though, the perfume or whatever just closes up my nose and throat. I wouldn't have a voice out here."

She smiled. "What really impressed me is that you did this for Tanya Brand, a made-up name from an old TV show, and not for Gemma Vereker the celebrity."

The two were so busy beaming at each other that they

never noticed Babs Basset passing behind, giving them a poisonous glare. Oddly, Liza realized, the real venom seemed directed toward Fergus.

Did Fergus of Scotland and Babs of the Sonoma Beach Bassets have some history?

Charley Ormond would be delighted—another subplot for her reality TV show.

A couple of hours later, Liza headed for the Skye Room, Rancho Pacificano's main ballroom. She'd spent part of that time acting as referee when Michael arrived to find Kevin ensconced at the resort. Liza also managed to fit in a light meal—sudoku solving was not improved by doing it to empty-belly music. Being overfull and having to go to the john was not a good idea, either.

Everything in moderation, Liza told herself as she joined the knot of people outside the main entrance. Charley Ormond's people had set up two tall folding chairs for the makeup department in a side corridor. Liza submitted to having a bib tied around her neck and a quick brushing across her face. "We don't have to go crazy," the makeup person told her. "They won't really be making any close-ups."

"Right," Liza said. "This is just to soak up the sweat."

The makeup brush froze in midair. "I thought this was just doing puzzles."

"They didn't tell you about the push-ups in between?" Liza took pity on the young woman's worried confusion. "Sorry, just joking. That's how my nerves show up."

"Better that than sweating." The girl removed the bib. "You're done."

Liza got out of the chair while a deeply suspicious Ian Quirk climbed in.

"Sure you're not going to find this a distraction?" Liza asked.

He gave her an icy glare. "When I concentrate, everything—*everything* recedes into the background."

"Then why raise so much hell at those other tournaments?"

Quirk gave her a twitch of a smile. "To psyche out the other players—like you."

She turned to one of the production assistants. "Where do I go next?"

The PA nodded to a man standing by the door with a clipboard. "The security manager, Mr. Roche, took care of seating the other contestants. Each of you has a reserved seat at the edge of the room, beside the gallery."

Liza glanced over with a half-smile. The guy stood at attention, a clipboard in his hands, just like the hall monitors used to do in grammar school. The smile faded, though, as she came closer. It wasn't just Roche's stance that was rigid. His tall, lean figure seemed to have been constructed during a skin shortage. A freckled, bald dome stretched over buzz-cut white bristles as if Roche had grown right through his hair. His face had all the mobility of a clenched fist.

The clipboard shot up as she approached. "You are?" Roche asked.

"Liza Kelly."

The security man gave a brief nod. "You'll be third to enter. We're doing it alphabetically."

Which, oddly enough, allows Babs Basset to come in first—and Gemma Vereker to be the grand finale entrance, Liza thought.

"Mr. Singleton will announce you, and I'll escort you to your seat."

Liza just hoped he wasn't going to clamp a hand on her arm. How long would it take her writing hand to recover from having its blood supply cut off?

The entrance went smoothly enough. Babs went in like a queen nodding to her subjects. Roy Conklin looked horrified at being in the spotlight. Liza got to her seat without falling on her face. She quickly spotted her own little entourage. Mrs. H.'s silly hat wobbled as if it were about to go aloft thanks to her vigorous clapping. At least neither Michael nor Kevin started hooting or making animal noises.

Somebody had been clever in relation to the name of the ballroom. The ceiling two stories above had been painted into a good trompe l'oeil rendition of the sky— but not the typical Technicolor overhead display of California. The background blue had a slightly steely cast, and the clouds were a bit grayer, edged with a rosy glow as if sunlight had managed to pass through. It reminded Liza of some days up in Oregon—or she guessed, in Scotland.

Down on the ground level, the room was set out with row after row of tables. Even with the seats set well apart, there had to be room for more than three hundred people. It might have been a big dinner, except that instead of place settings, each participant had a pair of pencils and pens, a scratch pad, and . . . Liza had to smile as she settled into her seat. *So goody bags have made their way from the Oscars and the Sundance Festival to the West Coast Sudoku Summit,* she thought.

She would have liked to check it out, but she heard the sharp sound of a chair scraping on the floor and turned to see Ian Quirk taking his place at the table behind her.

He glanced up, not so much interested in the painted sky as the camera crew established on the balcony above them. "Two for the price of one," he sneered. "How frugal."

Liza didn't get a chance to respond. Almost immediately, Will Singleton began running over the rules. The stuff on the tables represented all the aid the contestants could expect—no mechanical help, cell phones, or other paraphernalia allowed. This first puzzle represented an elimination round—Will was quite up front, warning that he expected the majority of people in the room would not finish by the time limit. Those who did finish in time would be ranked and participate in four more rounds—a morning and afternoon puzzle both on Saturday and

Sunday. The person with the highest overall ranking would win the prize.

Staffers began passing out sealed envelopes while Will whipped the cover off the large, remarkably ugly digital timer that apparently accompanied him to every tournament. The timer's display already blinked at 45.

"This represents your time limit," Will said. "Please open your puzzle envelopes . . . now."

Liza opened the envelope and scowled at the puzzle revealed within.

As she scanned the sparse array of numbers, she quickly saw that the first two of her Twelve Steps to Sudoku Mastery weren't going to work—there were no hidden singles or naked singles to be found.

Will wasn't kidding, she thought. *That usually means a pretty tough puzzle.*

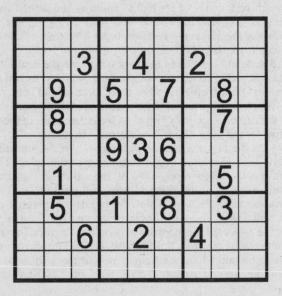

Grimly, she picked up a pencil and began listing the candidates, the possible answers for each space. Some squares got quite crowded. Those empty rows and columns meant that some spaces had six or even seven possibilities. Still, she kept at work until the full picture emerged.

Then Liza started scanning the subgrids across the top of the puzzle. The top right-hand box had a 2 in Row 2. That eliminated 2s in that grid and along the second row. The upper-left-hand box had 2s listed among the possibilities in both Row 1 and Row 3. The top center box had 2s only in Row 1. That meant that Row 3 was the only valid place to look for 2s in the upper-left-hand subgrid. Also, it meant that Liza could eliminate the 2s in the spaces in the first row of the box.

Three down, two hundred and some to go, she told herself. Scanning onward, she saw that the top three spaces on the second column were the only ones that held 6s. That eliminated three more 6s in Column 1 of the upper-left-hand subgrid.

Smiling silently, Liza hunted on.

Twenty-five minutes later, she finished tracing her third swordfish, a pattern of either-or choices regarding the placing of 9s across six spaces in the grid. It allowed her to remove five 9s from other spaces . . .

The sudden noise from behind shattered Liza's concentration. She glanced around to see Ian Quirk standing at his place. Damn! Had he finished the puzzle already? Maybe those Vegas people knew what they were talking about, saying he'd come in first.

Liza felt a stab of annoyance. Still, did he have to make such a production out of it? As she glared at him, it began to dawn on her that maybe Ian's face wasn't flushed with triumph.

His right hand clutched at his throat and his left waved wildly as he wobbled on his feet, making choking noises.

So much for not trying to psyche people out, Liza thought sourly. *Well, if he's giving us a sample of Ian Quirk's Allergy*

Theater, he's really hamming it up. I mean, who would believe such an over-the-top—

Her critique was interrupted as Ian dropped to the floor in convulsions.

4

"Ohmigod!" Liza leapt to her feet, staring down at Ian Quirk. The painful-looking contortions of his body didn't look like faking anymore. The question was, what to do about it?

Liza wasn't sure, and to judge from the babble of voices rising ever louder around her, nobody else seemed to know, either. A lot of people couldn't even see the twisting figure on the floor—they were yelling to find out what was going on.

A tall, skinny figure pushed through the growing circle around Quirk. Oliver Roche tossed the clipboard from his hand and pulled Ian away from the furniture into the open aisle—and also out of view of the camera on the gallery above.

Roche's voice rose in a shout over the hubbub. "Someone call 911." Dropping to one knee, he pulled out a handkerchief, folded it into a thick wad, and put it between the twitching man's lips. Then he moved Quirk onto his side. "He may vomit," Roche warned.

He looked up at the surrounding crowd. "Does anyone know if he's an epileptic?"

Liza spoke up, surprised at how tentative her voice sounded. "He's supposed to have allergies."

Roche shot to his feet. "Anyone on the phone to 911?"

An answer came out of the crowd.

"Tell them to hurry the ambulance. This may be a case of anaphylactic shock."

He dropped back down again, feeling for a pulse, and got on the phone himself.

It seemed like forever before Fergus Fleming burst through the doors, leading a team of paramedics.

They quickly loaded Quirk onto a gurney. Liza couldn't help seeing the grim expressions as the ambulance team wheeled him off.

Fleming glared up at the cameras aiming down at the stretcher team, obviously not delighted with this kind of publicity for his resort.

"Ladies—gentlemen!" Liza barely heard Will Singleton over the buzz of the crowd. Then Charley Ormond appeared beside him with a microphone, and his voice blared from the public-address system. "EXCUSE ME!"

That shut up most of the contestants.

Will continued a little less emphatically, "This is a terrible occurrence. I hope Mr. Quirk will be all right. We must also face the fact that this round of competition has been interrupted." He pointed to the digital timer, which continued to count down the seconds.

"That's unfair to those of us who didn't allow ourselves to be distracted!" Babs Basset climbed onto a chair, her puzzle in hand.

I guess some people are so self-absorbed, you'd have to set a bomb off under them to get their attention, Liza thought.

Will looked unhappily at the cameras recording this impromptu debate. Charley leaned forward. "We've already cut the sound and gone to the news desk. That will hold for a couple of minutes, but we need something to cover if this round is canceled. How about the promotional bit we were going to do? The Cirque de Soleil people are ready."

Will nodded. "You just need the puzzle."

Charley turned to Fergus Fleming. "And the fax machine."

He led her off as Kevin and Michael came through the crowd like a two-man flying wedge, Mrs. H. trailing behind them. "What was that all about?" she asked.

"I'm really not sure," Liza admitted.

Meanwhile, Will tried to reestablish control over the circus. "If you'd kindly return to your seats."

"Excuse me, but I don't think that's a good idea." Oliver Roche came out of the crowd, his clipboard at the ready. "I think everyone should clear the room in case the police want to examine the scene."

"Why would they want to do that?" Scottie Terhune burst out. "I mean, it was just an accident."

Roche whipped round, and for a second Liza thought he was going to lash out at Scottie with his trusty clipboard.

"Well, Mr. Roche is the security manager. Perhaps we should do as he suggests," Will said.

Babs Basset still complained loudly. Gemma Vereker headed for the doors without a word. Scottie Terhune just shrugged and, like most of the puzzle solvers, followed the movie star. Liza looked up. All of a sudden, the Skye Room's imitation blue sky looked more like a storm on the way.

Roche consulted his seating plan and started calling out names, including Liza's. "You were all seated closest to Mr. Quirk. I'd like you to tell me what you observed."

Liza shrugged at her friends and joined the tail end of the exodus. Once outside, she joined the knot of people around Oliver Roche, who was already locking the doors.

A short, potbellied guy in shorts and a T-shirt stepped up to complain. "I don't know why you had to chase us out of there. You wouldn't even let us bring anything. I mean, the guy just keeled over. Maybe the puzzle was too much for him. It was for me. I figured I'd at least last the first couple of rounds, but that Singleton guy started out with a killer."

Roche loomed over the complainer. Then, if anything, the muscles in his face tightened further. "What's that on your breath?"

"Hey," said Potbelly, "no need to get offensive."

Roche shook his head in exasperation. "It smells like peanuts."

"Well, yeah. I pretty much gave up on the puzzle. So I checked out the goody bag and found some candy."

Oliver Roche began rapidly paging through the contents of his clipboard. "The guest packages included Mr. Singleton's latest sudoku book in paperback, samples of quality toiletries, fragrances for both men and women, and imported chocolates and caramels. No peanut products."

The potbellied complainer shrugged. "I found a bunch of those little foil-wrapped, chocolate-covered Peanut Pellets."

Roche drew himself up. "The Rancho Pacificano would never include an item you could find at your local food mart."

Potbelly shrugged. "Well, maybe they were new and improved in dark chocolate. I dunno. I just ate them."

The security man began making the rounds of the other supposed eyewitnesses, sniffing their breath. "Did you have candy? Did you?"

"No," Liza told the nose thrusting at her mouth. "I was working on the puzzle. The first hint I had that anything was out of the ordinary was when Ian pushed his chair back."

Quite a few of the others, however, had just been marking time and enjoying a snack. Roche's jaw tightened so much, little Popeye muscles appeared in his cheeks. He shot a sudden glance at Liza. "You said he had allergies."

"To what, I couldn't say," Liza told him. "I just know that in the past he'd disrupted other tournaments, complaining that the arrangements weren't healthy." She took a deep breath. "But he also told me that he used threats like that as a sort of psychological warfare."

Roche pulled out his cell phone. Whoever he wanted to talk to, he had the number on speed dial. "Pete? Oliver Roche here. Did you hear about the guest collapsing at the hotel? Yeah, I expected you would. Look, could you come down here for a quick look around? I found some things that don't seem kosher. There's a good chance someone apparently tampered with the gift packages, introducing contraband that may have had a bad effect on this guy."

He glanced at Liza. "Apparently he wasn't exactly popular . . . but he was expected to win this tournament. No, I secured the scene. Thanks, Pete, I appreciate it."

Roche closed his phone and looked around at the people he'd been questioning. "Please don't go far. For one thing, I expect Mr. Singleton will be making some sort of announcement about a makeup puzzle or whatever. Also, Detective Janacek of the local police may want to speak with you."

The group broke up, Liza heading for her friends, who stood nearby.

"Well, that was kind of intense," Kevin said.

"Are you all right, dear?" Mrs. H. inquired anxiously.

Michael, however, was less impressed. "Is this the OC, or the OCD?" he asked. "The guy's trying to make a deep, dark mystery where there isn't any. I expect those goody bags weren't stuffed in a NASA white room, and the people doing the work were probably volunteers or hotel workers. It's not exactly a situation where it's unheard of for expensive candy to go missing and something cheaper to get substituted. Maybe the house dick over there should go sticking his nose in the staff's faces, looking for chocolate breath."

"One good thing," Kevin said. "If he's too sick to go on, one of your major competitors is out of the game."

"You wouldn't say that if you'd been closer when he went down," Liza told him. "It was pretty scary. I don't know what would have happened if Mr. Roche hadn't stepped in."

She turned to Mrs. H. "Did you happen to hear what they're showing instead of the first round of puzzle solving?" Not for the first time, she wished she'd been able to come down for the orientation day on Thursday. Unfortunately, Liza's schedule just hadn't allowed for that.

"The guy in the *Star Trek* shirt said he was trying to arrange something," Michael replied.

As if on cue, Scottie Terhune came down the hallway with Fergus Fleming, wheeling a large-screen television on a metal cart. Shambling along behind them came a weedy-looking guy whose staff uniform didn't seem to fit him right.

Once in the AV squad, always in the AV squad, Liza thought as the geeky-looking guy knelt, using some sort of tool to open an inconspicuous plate set in the baseboard. Seconds later, he had the set plugged in and a cable running to a connector in the wall.

A picture blossomed on the screen with the SINN logo in the lower-right corner and the words LIVE FROM IRVINE, CA running across the bottom. The picture itself showed the blank wall of a medium-sized office tower, covered with what seemed to be one of those fabric billboards bearing an enormous version of the network's logo.

"That's the SINN headquarters over in Irvine," Scottie explained.

As he spoke, the huge swath of fabric began to fall like a furling sail, and small human figures appeared, traveling down the expanse of revealed concrete in strangely dreamlike bounds. Liza gasped, then realized the people must be wearing some sort of tethers and that these were controlled falls, a sort of vertical ballet.

Vaguely, she remembered Charley Ormond making some comment about Cirque de Soleil.

Meanwhile, the logo covering had dropped out of sight, revealing a familiar nine-by-nine gridwork painted on the wall. In this case, though, each space probably took up more square footage than Liza's whole house back home in Maiden's Bay.

The vertical dancers moved into boxes, and numbers began to appear. The tethered performers must have had extra-large cans of spray paint. They'd go flying up, then come bounding down again, like spiders creating a very mathematical web indeed.

Liza ran a professional eye over the developing puzzle. Will wasn't out to eliminate anyone here. This looked to be a simple puzzle, solvable by people with only rudimentary sudoku skills.

Even as the top row of subgrids took form, she spotted a hidden single that would let a solver place a 6 immediately.

Well, it was supposed to be a promo. People would be able to see it from miles away, and they should be able to solve it. She smiled, appreciating a publicity coup for SINN, for Will, and for the West Coast Sudoku Summit.

Liza glanced at her companions. Mrs. Halvorsen stared, entranced, sighing, "Oh, my."

Kevin tried to be more practical. "That had to set them back a few bucks."

Not to be outdone, Michael aimed a critical frown at the screen. "Didn't Microsoft use a stunt like this a couple of years ago to launch Vista?"

Liza said nothing as she watched the second set of three rows take shape. The flying sign painters must have done some intensive practice to create numerals so quickly. Especially, Liza realized, since they were essentially doing the job blind. Charley Ormond had only faxed the final puzzle to the crew at headquarters mere moments ago.

The aerialists leapfrogged down to paint clues into the final three rows of the gargantuan puzzle. Hardly had they begun, though, when a gasp ran through most of the people watching.

Mrs. H. turned confused eyes to Liza. "What's the matter?"

But Liza felt too sick to explain. All that money, time, and talent . . . and in the end it was all for nothing.

Michael, the other sudoku fanatic in their little group,

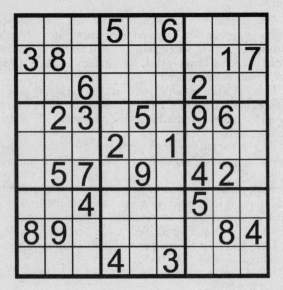

spoke up to explain. "They made a mistake in the puzzle. The rules forbid having the same numbers in any row or column. But look at that second-to-last row."

Liza saw it only too clearly. The two 8s were separated by a good half a block's distance. But they were still too close for a legal sudoku.

5

"Pardon." Liza felt herself elbowed to the side as Charley Ormond shoved her way to the front of the crowd, a cell phone to her ear.

"How many calls is that? And they all say the same thing?" Charley's Strine accent got much stronger when she got agitated. "Yes, sir, I'm in front of the screen now. They're complaining that there are two eights, and that's a mistake. Where? Mmm-hmm."

She stared for a moment at the screen. "Is it possible that the painting teams might have gotten confused—ah, you have the fax right there. And that's the source of the error."

The newswoman stood silent for a moment, her perky features tightening and going red as the executive on the other end of the phone connection vented his displeasure. "No, sir, I don't have an explanation." Her voice got a bit grimmer as she went on. "But I intend to get one."

By now, Will Singleton had made his way to the screen, staring in bafflement at the enormous disaster. "We were working to reschedule the first round when I heard about these telephone calls."

Charley Ormond rounded on him. "Can you account for that—that—?"

"Oversized mistake?" Babs Basset sweetly suggested. She came over and patted Will on the arm. "How unfortunate for you. But I suppose that's the drawback when you insist on being a one-man show. There's no one to catch the little problems before they become big ones."

Boy, if there was an Oscar for fake sympathy, she'd be a lock. Liza silently marveled at Babs's performance. Then again, she realized, there was already enough of that at the awards show anyway.

Will continued to look at the screen. "I can't claim to remember every detail of every puzzle I've created," he said. "But I seem to recall that the third clue in that row should be a three. That would set up a hidden single in the lower-left-hand box, you see."

"Well, I've been assured it was an eight on the fax that went to Irvine," Charley said.

The two numbers are pretty similar," Will suggested. One might be mistaken for the other if the fax wasn't clear."

"Let's see the original—I gave it back to you," Charley said.

"Certainly." Will rummaged in his portfolio, brought out a sheet of paper, and stared in dismay. "It—uh—"

Charley looked at the puzzle and shook her head. "It appears to have two eights."

Will looked so bewildered—and embarrassed—that Liza's heart just about broke.

"I can't understand it," he said in a low voice. "I printed it out of the computer—"

"You're using computer-generated sudoku for this tournament?" Babs just about proclaimed it at the top of her lungs.

Will's face reddened behind his salt-and-pepper beard. "I create all of my sudoku by hand," he almost snarled. "But I check them on the computer. That's why I can't understand how it returned a puzzle that manifestly could not work."

He turned to Charley. "Changing that second eight into a three would solve the problem."

She looked about ready to bite his head off. "Well, it would solve one problem. Of course the wall-dancing team only has black paint—they didn't know they'd have to white out part of their work. And there's that little snag of a nationwide television audience watching us screw up the whole presentation."

Now Will looked just about crushed.

Before Babs could get another dig in, Oliver Roche appeared with a thick-bodied, gray-haired man who had a gold badge dangling from the breast pocket of his suit jacket.

"I asked Detective Janacek to come down," Roche said. "But he has an important announcement to make."

The detective looked around with watery blue eyes. "I called the hospital before I left the station. They told me that Mr. Quirk never responded to treatment. He was declared dead in the emergency room—anaphylactic shock. Among other things, it turns out he was extremely allergic to peanuts."

The tournament participants stood silent in disbelief.

Liza shook her head, remembering what Ian Quirk had said while he was sitting in the makeup chair. He'd icily bragged about the strength of his concentration, how he could make everything around him recede from whatever task he was doing.

It seemed as though his boast turned out to be fatally true. Quirk must have been concentrating on the puzzle so intensely that he never noticed the telltale, dangerous odor of peanuts until the allergen had already affected him.

"Now Mr. Roche raised some disturbing points," Janacek went on, "so I thought I should come and take a look."

Using Roche's seating list, he gathered the people who

had been near Ian Quirk, asking questions of the potbellied guy and the others, including Liza.

Then he turned to the crowd at large. "Did any of you folks take a look inside those gift bags?"

Several people made shamefaced confessions that they'd gotten in over their heads with the competition puzzle and had turned instead to check out their goodies.

Most of them, however, found no peanut products, just the VIP luxury items that Oliver Roche had described when he sealed off the Skye Room.

When Janacek asked for names from the people who did find peanuts, Roche checked them against his seating plan—and found they all were near Quirk.

The more the police detective listened, the less happy he looked. Liza had watched Roche make the call to the police. He'd used speed dial for a direct number, and greeted Janacek by his first name. The cop had come over to the Rancho Pacificano as a personal favor. Now it began to look like some sort of case—and worse, a case taking place in front of TV cameras.

Charley Ormond proceeded to turn that thought into the absolute worst-case scenario, reappearing with a camera crew at her heels.

"Is it true that Ian Quirk's tragic death may not have been an accident?" she asked, all perky interest.

Janacek was too old a fish to be hooked that way. "There seem to be some unexplained circumstances involved with this incident," he said. Then his voice grew more cautious. "I was invited in an unofficial capacity to come and observe."

Sure, Liza thought, *whoever runs Homicide would be just delighted to have one of the squad's detectives going out to drum up some extra business.*

"And have you found . . ." Charley eagerly followed up, but Janacek held up a hand.

"I can't comment, except to say that we're about to examine the scene." He gestured for Roche to open the ball-

room door and firmly closed it behind them. Liza heard
the click of the lock.

Not one to be deterred by a lack of facts, Charley advanced on Liza. "Ms. Kelly, you have a certain reputation
for solving mysteries as well as sudoku puzzles. Can you
comment on this strange development?"

"I'm sure I can't add anything to what Detective Janacek said," Liza carefully replied.

"Ian Quirk was seated directly behind you, wasn't he?"
Charley pressed.

Liza heard the implied challenge in that question and
answered with just the facts. "I heard him rise rather
abruptly. When I turned, he had a hand at his throat, apparently in some distress. Then he collapsed. At this point,
that's all I know. And I'm sure if you ask any of the other
people who were nearby, that's pretty much what they'd all
have to say."

Before Charley could frame another question, the doors
opened, and Janacek's voice came from inside. "I'm calling this in. Maybe planting peanuts all around this guy
was only supposed to make him sick. But there is such a
thing as overkill."

Charley Ormond immediately repositioned her camera
crew to catch Janacek as he came out. Liza took advantage
of the distraction to head for the elevator and the safety of
her room. Michael, Kevin, and Mrs. Halvorsen caught on
immediately, following in silence.

Once inside, they filled the two chairs and the small
couch in the suite's sitting room.

"Before you even ask, I'm not playing detective on this,"
Liza told them emphatically. "For one thing, I didn't even
like Ian Quirk."

"I could name at least one other person you didn't like—
but you still found their killer," Mrs. H. pointed out.

"Ava Barnes will probably tell you it's necessary to promote your column," Kevin chimed in.

"Not to mention what the Dragon Lady will say."

Michael used his only semijoking nickname for Michelle Markson. The room phone rang. "What do you bet that's her?"

As soon as Liza picked up the receiver, she could hear Michelle's crisp tones. "I understand that collapse I saw on SINN is now being considered a suspicious death."

Liza stood silent. How did Michelle find out this stuff? And damn Michael for being right!

"And hello to you, too, Michelle," she said.

"Do you have that laptop I gave you?" Michelle asked.

"Why, uh, yes." Liza had brought it along in case peace and quiet got too quiet. She could always compose a new column or two.

"Excellent. I'll e-mail you all our background files on the tournament's major players."

Liza found herself staring at the phone. "You assembled background info on a bunch of sudoku people?" she asked, dumbfounded.

"Keeping files on teammates and major competitors is standard procedure for our sports clients," Michelle pointed out. "Although you're not a client per se, I thought it would be a good idea to assemble some information when you agreed to go into this competition. And given this strange talent you've displayed, I thought the information might have a practical use."

Liza knew the "strange talent" Michelle just mentioned had nothing to do with sudoku.

"Michelle," she said, "I have no intention—"

Michelle cut her off. "Dear, I've seen this often enough now to know what will happen. Your lips will tell me 'No, no, no,' and then you'll end up digging into the matter."

"Someday I'll surprise you," Liza replied.

"My dear Liza," her partner replied. "You and I both know that in this business, surprises are the last things we want. Ysabel has uploaded the files, in case you decide you need them."

Translation: *when* you decide you need them.

Michelle suddenly shifted mental gears. "Please recall!

that you have a client down there. You wouldn't want this situation to harm Gemma professionally—or personally."

"Gemma's fine," Liza told her partner. "She even helped to lead everyone away from the—" She paused. No, there was no other way to put it. "From the crime scene."

"I'm glad to hear it. And, oh, yes." Now Michelle's voice took on a studied offhand manner. "Buck Foreman should be there within the hour, traffic allowing."

Further translation: Liza had about sixty minutes to stop dithering and get to work. Buck Foreman wasn't just a private investigator, he was also a physically impressive guy. He wouldn't exactly appreciate Liza wasting his time.

Sighing with defeat, Liza said, "Well, I guess I'll see Buck then."

Michelle cut the connection, and Liza got up to plug her laptop into the wall. "You're not going to believe what Michelle is sending."

Michael got in front of the computer while Mrs. Halvorsen smiled. "I'll enjoy seeing that nice Mr. Foreman again."

"In the meantime, I guess we'd better try to make some sense of what's going on here," Liza said.

"I never realized there were so many local sudoku experts." Kevin squinted over Michael's shoulder at the computer screen. "Each of these people seems to be the top dog in a different town."

" 'There can be only one.' " Michael quoted one of his favorite movies in his most oracular tones. "Or maybe it's more like the Mafia," he went on in a normal voice, glancing over at Liza. "Would that make you the don of Portland?"

Michael might have been kidding, but Kevin frowned in thought. "You know, Quirk came from Las Vegas, which is kind of a Mob town. He was involved in the gambling business. Suppose he ran afoul of some organized crime type?"

"If he was going to get whacked, you'd expect the cause of death to be a bullet in the head, probably in a parking garage, not peanut fumes in a sudoku tournament," Michael objected. "I think we'll have to go through the whole MOM thing once again."

"That's Motive, Opportunity, and Means," Liza explained, catching a puzzled look from Mrs. Halvorsen.

"Specifically," Liza went on, "I want to concentrate on opportunity. Why here? Why now?"

"The policeman said the trick with the peanuts might have been aimed at making that poor man sick," Mrs. H. suggested. "Maybe the idea was just to get him out of the contest."

"Quirk was favored to take first prize," Liza said.

"And there's the motive." Mrs. Halvorsen's nod was emphatic, even without her silly hat to point it up. "Someone else wants that prize money."

"Or needs it," Michael said, flicking back and forth between file windows on the computer screen. "That would let you out, Liza. Between your partnership in Michelle's agency and your column, you've got to be sitting pretty."

"Doing well enough to pass along the reward connected to your last case." Kevin nodded at Liza, bringing a shade of pink to Mrs. Halvorsen's face as the beneficiary of her neighbor's generosity.

"What about the others?" Liza asked, a little embarrassed herself.

Michael skimmed the screen. "Well, Barbara Basset navigated her way through three marriages, picking up enough along the way to at least aspire to a high-class lifestyle."

"Well, of course. She's one of the Sonoma Beach Bassets." Liza mimicked that haughty voice.

"You know," Kevin said, "if you sort of slur those words together, you get a pretty good description of her, too."

"Sonomabeachbasset," Liza murmured, then laughed.

"Roy Conklin teaches at the university level," Michael went on. "He's a tenured professor with a fairly modest salary, but no family—and he lives within his means. Then we have Sylvester Terhune."

"Is this the guy in the *Star Trek* shirt?" Kevin asked. "I

think I see why he prefers to have people call him Scottie."

Michael turned away from the computer. "You could also call him broke. He had a good personnel job at a big company but lost it three months ago after a major merger. And he has an expensive condo to pay for. Apparently, he's been on eBay and a lot of other web locations, selling off what appears to be an extensive *Trek* collection."

"That won't last forever," Kevin said.

Mrs. Halvorsen nodded. "He could really use the prize money."

"But—Scottie?" Liza shook her head. "He's the most upbeat, easygoing person at this tournament."

And one of the few sudoku professionals I really like, she added silently.

Shrugging, Michael went back to the screen. "According to these rough financials, your friend Will Singleton has made a pretty good living off sudoku. Book deals, personal appearances, syndicated puzzles in newspapers and magazines, other media tie-ins—"

"And there's his connection with SINN," Kevin put in.

Liza suddenly found herself remembering Ian Quirk's jibe at Will, calling him a media whore. Of course, Ian and Babs were both angling for some sort of deal with SINN, too.

From Will's point of view, eliminating Ian Quirk from the tournament might allow for a dark horse winner and more publicity—as well as dealing Quirk a humiliating setback.

Would Will be just as glad to eliminate Quirk on a more permanent basis?

Reluctantly, Liza shared that information. She tried to find other motives or means in the downloaded material, but they kept coming back to money and power.

"Well, those are the classic motivations for murder," Michael pointed out.

Liza drifted over to the balcony door, staring out at the harbor below. "Along with revenge and jealousy," she finally said. "What if there's a bigger picture we're not see-ing?"

"Like what?" Kevin asked.

"Like damaging the whole tournament," Liza re-sponded. "The leading contestant becomes deathly ill, the big promotional event goes disastrously off the rails . . ."

"I think that was a mistake," Mrs. Halvorsen said.

"Yes, a mistake and an accident—except the accident turned out to be fatal."

"Boy, you love your conspiracy theories." Michael laughed. "So who's behind the dastardly deeds, the Cross-word Lovers Cabal, the International Alliance of Word Search Fanatics?"

"I was thinking more of Babs Basset," Liza admitted. "From the moment I first saw her, she's been giving Will a hard time, moaning about the whole tournament. Maybe she figures that she should be the queen bee of any West Coast tournaments. You should have seen the look on her face when Gemma Vereker showed up and suddenly got all the media attention."

"Well, at least it's a different motive," Mrs. H. com-mented.

"And something else we can run past Buck Foreman." Liza looked at her watch. "Maybe we should get back downstairs and catch him before he gets sucked into the whole tournament mob scene."

They managed to intercept Buck at the entrance to the main hotel building, but there was no way to insulate him from the chattering crowd. Big and hard-looking, the pri-vate eye glanced around with the poker face of an anthro-pologist studying a particularly bizarre tribe of primitives.

"Y'know," Buck said, "this reminds me of a surveil-lance case I had a while back. I followed the subject to a hotel in the middle of a chess tournament. The moment we came into the lobby, all the players were bragging about how well they did."

For just a second, his face lightened to a grin. "Chess nuts boasting in an open foyer."

Mrs. H. laughed, Kevin winced, and Michael actually said, "Ouch!"

"Don't ever let Michelle catch you saying something like that," Liza warned, smiling. "She considers puns to be the lowest form of humor."

Buck shrugged. "It's just an idiosyncrasy that she has to put up with."

Not for the first time, Liza found herself wondering about the exact relationship between her partner and the PI. Certainly, there was a business component. Whenever a client got in trouble or Michelle needed leverage against a studio or management, Buck went out to beat the bushes or dig under rocks and get the goods. Other times, though, Buck would drop off the radar—and the usually hyperconnected Michelle went incommunicado.

Right now, though, Liza had a different mystery to deal with. She quickly outlined what had happened to Ian Quirk and the fiasco with the promotional event, then went down the possible suspects and their motivations.

Buck whipped out a notebook and jotted away. "Nice summary, Kelly. I hope this motive stuff helps to narrow things down." He flipped the notebook closed. "Otherwise, the cops will have to spread the net pretty wide." He cast an expert eye over the crowd. "What have you got here, a couple hundred people?"

"More like three hundred," Liza replied. "Not counting the staff."

"Just imagine the fingerprinting." Buck gave a little shudder. "So where did it happen?"

Liza led him to the Skye Room. The doors were open now, showing a dozen police—uniformed, plainclothes, and technicians—processing the area. Dashing around at the fringes, clipboard still in hand, was Oliver Roche.

Buck stared, then gave a short bark of laughter. "So this is where the Roach ended up."

PART TWO:
Fuzzy Logic

"Forging chains of logic" sounds very impressive, but a lot of sudoku solving depends on the homely process of elimination. If a 7 appears in this space, it prohibits the appearance of a 7 somewhere else.

That's why I'm especially fond of the technique called row and box/column and box interactions. This involves scanning three-space segments of a column or row as divided by the subgrids in a sudoku.

We're not looking for a particular space, but rather for a clump of spaces containing a particular digit among the candidates. Say we're looking for 2s in the middle tier of boxes, Rows 4 through 6. The bottom row has a 2 in the third box, eliminating 2s in the end segments of Rows 4 and 5 and throughout Row 6. Row 4 has six 2s in its remaining segments, but Row 5 has only two, both of them in the second box. That means 2 can only appear in those two spaces in the row, and the three 2s in the segment above in Row 4 can be eliminated.

It's sort of like scientists trying to track down a subatomic particle. They might not know exactly where it is, but they have a firm idea where it's not.

—Excerpt from *Sudo-cues* by Liza K

6

Liza stopped dead in her tracks. "You mean you know that man?"

Buck gave her a grimly amused smile. "In certain circumstances, Oliver the Roach is almost legendary. He was the most miserable mother—"

He gave a sudden cough, glancing over at Mrs. H. "As I was saying, he was the most miserable mother's son on the LAPD, living proof that psych tests don't weed out all the head cases in the academy."

"So he was—" Michael began.

"Let's just say if you looked up 'piece of work' in the dictionary, you'd find the Roach's portrait." Foreman shook his head. "Anyone who gets a police shield expects to exert some authority—it's part of the job. But some people take it to extremes. I wonder if Roche ever regretted that he was so skinny—he acted as if he'd have liked to be one of those Southern sheriffs, ramming his big belly into people to shove them around."

"He had a heavy hand?" Kevin asked.

"And not just with civilians. He was a complete control freak—drove his partners crazy. They'd do anything to

escape. I can't swear that some of these aren't just cop stories, but I heard of one guy who shot himself in the foot to
get away. Then there was the female partner who trumped
up harassment charges."

"He really does sound like a—what did you call him? A
piece of work?" Mrs. Halvorsen said.

"So why did he give up the police force?" Michael asked.
"He can't have completely exhausted the partner pool."

"No, but he finally exhausted the patience of the big
brass," Buck said. "He was convinced some guy was the
perp on a case, and just about broke the guy's arm to prove
it. Turned out it was another guy altogether. There was a
good-sized stink, and Roche retired—ahem—'for health
reasons.'"

"You seem to know a great deal about that man." Mrs.
Halvorsen looked up at Buck with interest. "Were you ever
his partner?"

"Not exactly," Buck rumbled. "It just happened that his
bad behavior primed the pump with the media, starting
a whole 'the police are out of control' campaign. I was
testifying in a big case, and the defense lawyer brought up
something stupid I'd said years ago. But he had tape, he
caused a big commotion, got his client off—and when the
media lynching was done, I was out of a job."

"At least you're still investigating," Liza told him. "Look
where he ended up."

Buck shrugged. "Don't knock it. He's got a regular pay-
check, probably a pension—and his own little kingdom to
push people around in."

Liza found herself remembering Oliver Roche's propri-
etary way with the Skye Room. She looked up at Buck to
find him smiling slightly. "Once a cop, always a cop," he
said. "Roche is dying to get into this investigation." He
nodded into the room, where a young detective stood with
a notebook while Roche animatedly talked away. "They
finally detained one guy to take his statement so the rest of
them could do their jobs without Roche underfoot."

It seemed that ploy had worked as long as it could. Now

Detective Janacek came over to talk to Roche. The head of hotel security looked ready to try an argument, but the veteran cop got his way and even managed an affable handshake with Roche before sending him off.

"I wonder how long it's going to stay friendly," Buck muttered.

"What do you mean?" Michael asked.

"Like I said, he's dying to get into this investigation. If he can't get in with the cops, he'll do it himself." Buck turned to face Liza and all her friends. "This is going to be a high-profile case—the SINN people will make sure of that. If Roche manages to solve it, he may not get his job back, but he could probably land an investigative job somewhere."

Roche proceeded to prove Buck right. He stepped out of the ballroom, his face so tight Liza suspected his teeth must be creaking. The first person he spotted was Babs Basset.

"Excuse me, ma'am," Roche said, stepping up to her. "I have a couple of questions—"

She stared down her nose at him as if an earthworm had suddenly addressed her. "Go away, you strange little man."

And even though Roche topped her by a head, he did slink off, just like some shlubby strange little man.

"Damn, she's good," Buck muttered.

Roche moved away quickly, scanning for some other person to question. Of course, he spotted Liza. And then he spotted Buck Foreman.

The security manager came straight at Liza, giving her the sort of squinty-eyed glare that Clint Eastwood used to specialize in. "I've heard about your reputation, Ms. Kelly," he said. "And let me warn you right now against injecting yourself into police business. That won't be tolerated here."

"Injecting?" Buck's eyebrows rose as if in mild surprise. "You mean the way you're doing?"

Liza thought that Oliver Roche's face was wrapped about as tight as humanly possible. Watching the man's

muscles contort at Buck's shot, she feared that Roche's
skull might implode.

"I maintain an excellent professional relationship with
the local police," he ground out. "I'm sure Detective Janacek will be glad for me to lend a hand."

Buck dropped his light approach. "Listen, Roche, you
ought to know there's a difference between telling old war
stories over a couple of beers and letting somebody inter-
fere on a big case. When you were on the job, would you
have done that, even for some retired guy?"

Roche growled deep in his throat. Then he spun on his
heel and stalked off.

"Well," Buck said, "I guess he didn't have an answer for
that."

Liza frowned. "But I don't think he's going to thank any
of us for witnessing it."

Will Singleton came darting out of the crowd, so distracted he was chewing one end of his beard. "Liza!" he
called as he came past. "I was just going to have someone
call you. We finally have the plans firmed up for the makeup
round."

He nodded at the police still in the Skye Room. "There's
no hope of getting the large room back in time. So we'll be
using all of the other event rooms. They're smaller, but
they should accommodate everyone."

"Sounds good to me," Liza said, "but I'm guessing
Charley Ormond is tearing her hair out, trying to spread
all her camera crews around."

Will sighed. "We're waiting to see whether she can get
some reinforcements," he admitted. "However that works
out, the firm time for the new round is six-thirty."

"I'll be there," Liza promised. She hesitated for a
second, then hooked Will's arm before he got away. "Er,
I want you to meet a friend of mine. This is Will
Singleton—"

Buck stuck out his hand. "Buck Foreman," he said,
shaking. "I was quite a fan of your crossword puzzles."

Will cast a glance at the chaos around him. "Some

days, I wonder if changing fields was a good idea. You're not here for the tournament, Mr. Foreman?"

"No, I'm just an old colleague of Liza's. We both worked at her agency," Buck said smoothly. "When I heard she was going to be in town . . . or at least, close by, I figured I'd try to get down and see her."

"That's very nice," Will said. "Good to meet you, Buck. Who knows? Maybe Liza can convert you to sudoku."

"I wouldn't bet on it," Liza told him. "But if it's okay with you, I'd like to show him around."

"I'm sure he won't be able to see us looking any worse," Will replied. Then someone else called his name, and he was off to fight another fire.

Liza followed him with her eyes. "After doing that, I feel like a real . . ."

"Detective?" Buck asked.

"I think 'turd' is more the word," she replied tartly. "Will is an old friend, and here I am—"

"Fingering him?" Mrs. H. suggested.

"Treating him like a suspect." Liza's words came out as an unhappy sigh. "It's the same thing with Scottie Terhune. He may be a bit loud, but at bottom I think he's a good guy. Roy Conklin is maybe a bit too much on the shy and quiet side, but he's harmless enough. Ian Quirk was probably the one I wouldn't mind giving the finger—"

"Excuse me?" Michael said.

"I mean he's—he *was*—the most annoying pseudo sudokologist I ever met," Liza tried to explain. "If I knew anything bad about him, I wouldn't have minded ratting him out."

She looked around in the crowd. "The next worst, at least here, would be Babs Basset, I think. Do you want me to introduce you to her, too?"

"And get the same look she gave Roche?" Buck shuddered. "Heaven forbid. If I ever have to face that particular gem of womanhood, I want to have something solid on her."

In the end, they circulated until Liza tracked down all

the other people who had some sort of motive. She even pointed out Fergus Fleming.

Finally, she looked at her watch. "I don't know if any of this was helpful. You came all the way down here because Michelle asked you to—"

"I know," Buck commiserated, "and I still haven't pointed at anyone and said, 'That's the one who done it.'"

"To tell the truth, I was wondering why you came," Michael admitted.

"For one thing, Liza is a friend," Buck replied. "And I think you're all off to some sort of start, although I have to admit I'm not really sure yet how to finish it. For another—well, sometimes it's easier to do what Michelle wants."

"No fooling," Liza and Michael both said almost simultaneously.

"So what will you do now?" Mrs. H. asked.

"Now I'll hit some sources and see what I can find out about these folks that isn't on the World Wide Web," Buck replied. "I suspect we'll be in touch, Liza, if either of us finds out anything else interesting."

"Right now, that seems like a big 'if' for us," Liza said.

"That's the way it always looks at the start of a case," Buck told her. "Now I know you'll want to do whatever it is you do to get ready for this rematch—"

"You make it sound like the World Wrestling Federation," Liza tried to joke. "But the fact is, I do need to decompress."

"And I have just the way to do it," Kevin jumped in.

"And what, exactly, is that?" was Michael's bristling response.

"A drive," Kevin went on as if Michael hadn't spoken. "I managed to rent this really amazing car, and I thought we could take it out for a little run."

"I've got a car," Michael objected. "Why can't I take Liza for a drive?"

"Because I asked first," Kevin replied.

Liza rolled her eyes. *Here we go again.*

"A drive might be nice—as long as you keep off the

freeways." Buck gloomily considered his own trip back to L.A.

Mrs. H. glanced back and forth between Liza's squabbling suitors. "Well, Kevin did ask first. I'll tell you what, though, Michael. Liza and I are supposed to go to this big dinner tonight. Why don't you take Liza." She turned to Kevin. "And you can take me someplace nice in this wonderful car of yours."

That managed to restore the peace. Buck headed for home, Liza zipped back to her room to freshen up, and Kevin went for his wonder-car.

Moments later, Liza came out the front entrance of the hotel to see a long, low, streamlined shape roll along the drive, engine thrumming. A tinted window rolled down on the passenger's side, and Kevin waved out at her. "What do you think?"

"A Porsche?" Liza said. "Very Hollywood."

"A Porsche Carrera 911." Kevin proudly expanded on the subject.

"This must have knocked you back a hefty amount, even for a weekend rental." Liza eased her way into the seat.

"When I saw it was available—well, I always wanted to drive a spy car."

"And they didn't tell you anything about how it would help you pick up girls?" Liza asked.

Kevin smoothly pulled away. "There may have been some mention of that."

Liza looked over her shoulder. "Not much room in the backseat there, though."

"I believe there's a dingus that lets the front seats go flat," Kevin said.

"Don't even think of it," Liza told him. "This is a rental car. Who knows what's gone on in here?"

From the look on his face, Kevin obviously hadn't thought of that.

"Don't worry," Liza tried to reassure him, "I think I have some hand sanitizer in my bag." She settled back in her seat to enjoy the view—and Newport Beach offered a lot to enjoy. Like any upscale Southern California town, the main drag had been landscaped within an inch of its life. Even the medians were manicured as they rolled past a very high-end mall in the obligatory Spanish colonial style.

Kevin drove on, then pulled into a gas station, impressing the resident motorheads as much with his female passenger as with his ride, Liza noticed with a grin. He had a moment of doubt and fear, looking for where the gas went in. The door for the fuel intake was in the right front fender, in front of Liza's seat. Kevin fumbled for a moment to get the door open. But he quickly unscrewed the gas cap and topped up the tank, and they resumed their progress.

"Thanks for showing me off, but now they'll know we're tourists," she told him.

"Because of the gas tank thing?" he asked.

Liza shook her head. "Because our windows were down. If you want to look like you belong around here, you have to use your air conditioner."

Kevin shrugged, tapping the button that brought the windows up. "By all means, let's look like natives." The AC came on with a blast of cold air that Kevin quickly moderated.

Now they were getting out of the more built-up area, climbing up into the hills, trying a little more speed on the emptier roads. Liza didn't talk, noting Kevin's concentration behind the wheel. Well, he was more used to an SUV. A sports car would be a more responsive, finicky beast . . .

The engine rumbled as Kevin accelerated up a long rise, then made a sharp left.

And then suddenly he was wrestling with the wheel as the Porsche went fishtailing along the pavement!

7

"What the—?" Kevin got no further, saving his breath for his battle against the Porsche's wild shimmy, his knuckles white as he gripped the steering wheel.

Liza clung to the dashboard, glad for her seat belt. The sports car seemed to buck back and forth as if it were trying to free itself of its passengers.

Liza had only encountered something like this once before. During a very cold snap back home in Oregon, she'd driven onto a patch of black ice coming home one night. Once experienced, the terrible feeling that your wheels weren't quite in contact with the road anymore stuck with you.

Somehow, though, encountering a patch of ice in Southern California in springtime seemed a bit unlikely.

At least the Porsche had chosen an empty stretch of road for its misbehavior. That was lucky, because they hurtled several times across the median line into the lane for oncoming traffic before Kevin got them straightened out and slowed down.

They slumped back in their seats as the car finally lurched to a stop. "Y'know, Kevin, if this was supposed to get me relaxed, I think you overdid it," Liza joked feebly as she unclamped her fingers.

"I don't know what you're talking about," Kevin replied. "I feel perfectly wrung out."

She laughed, then wrinkled her nose at a sharp odor wafting in with the chilly blast of the air-conditioning. "Is that gasoline?"

But hitting a standing puddle of gas in the road seemed just about as unlikely as black ice.

"I suppose we can wait until the cold sweat dries," Kevin said, "but if we want to allow you any time before that makeup round, we'd better get going—slowly and carefully."

He started up the car, and they retraced their steps at a sedate twenty-five miles an hour.

That didn't make much difference on the less frequented roads out in the boonies. But as they got back into Newport Beach, even the side streets had traffic.

Judging from the rising crescendo of car horns behind them, about half the motorists in California were expressing their frustration. When a guy in an old junker swerved around them with a derisive hoot, Kevin hung his head and kept grimly driving on.

After what seemed like forever, at last they reached the Rancho Pacificano property. The Porsche wasn't happy at being throttled back like this—they limped all the way down the long driveway.

Kevin pulled up in front of the hotel, and Liza got out. "Thanks, Kevin. Your intentions were good."

"Yeah," he said gloomily. "But the machinery wasn't. And now I suppose it's too late to go back to the dealership and have somebody look at this piece of—"

He huffed out an angry breath. "Forgive me if I don't see you before the competition. I think I might not be good luck."

Liza managed a laugh and headed inside. An improvised sign in the lobby gave a list of contestants and the event rooms where they were supposed to go. She looked long enough to find that she was scheduled for the Hebrides Room and then went up to her suite. When she entered, she saw that the door to Mrs. Halvorsen's bedroom was closed.

She must be taking a rest, Liza thought, tiptoeing to the bathroom. Taking a washcloth, she soaked it with cold water and held it to her face. Then Liza looked at her watch. She could lie down for half an hour and still have ample time to take a shower and gird her loins for the battle downstairs.

Recovered if not exactly rested, Liza headed back into the tournament madness.

The SINN makeup area was crammed into a side corridor leading to some maintenance and storage spaces. Liza got the same makeup artist, but this time there was no joking around. The young woman took a little more care with her brushes. "The cameras will be closer."

Liza nodded. This time, the camera crews wouldn't be inconspicuously shooting from a gallery. They'd be in her face.

She went through the double doors of the Hebrides Room to find the interior rearranged from a party space with a podium to a miniature version of the competition area in the ballroom. Long rows of tables arranged with staggered seating faced a single smaller table in the front of the room. Will Singleton's digital monstrosity had been replaced by what would normally be a wall clock showing the time as 6:20.

A volunteer conducted Liza into the room and led her to an aisle seat. As Liza looked around, she didn't see any particularly familiar faces. That was good. She'd feared Charley Ormond might persuade Will to create an all-star room to make her camerawork easier.

Something else registered—a good number of seats stood empty, which didn't seem likely given that the competition was supposed to start in minutes. Apparently some of the participants, having gotten one stiff taste of Singleton sudoku, had decided not to suffer through another.

Liza took her seat and checked the two pencils and pens waiting for her. She grinned. *I guess they decided there wouldn't be any goody bags this time around.*

One of the tournament volunteers stood in the front of the room and rehashed the rules. Then she distributed the puzzles in their sealed envelopes. By the time she was finished, the clock up front had almost reached the magic moment.

When the second hand indicated half-past six on the dot, the woman called out, "Please begin."

Liza grabbed a pencil, opened the envelope, removed the puzzle, and immediately began filling in candidates. Given the complexity of the last puzzle, trying out simpler techniques would simply waste time.

As soon as she had all the possibilities listed, Liza began the work of thinning them down. She used the interaction between subgrids to prune some 3s out of one column. Then she spotted a naked pair—two spaces in the same row that had the same two candidates. That meant one space had to hold the 1 and the other the 5, and all other examples of those digits in the row could be eliminated.

That was the easy stuff. Liza kept cycling through her dozen most dependable solving techniques, rising in complexity. She traced two X-wings, logical chains making a rectangular path across the grid work and establishing two pairs of possible answers for four spaces. One allowed her to remove three extraneous 7s. The other didn't eliminate anything.

Involved in tracing the possible logic of a swordfish chain, Liza suddenly became aware of movement behind her—how she couldn't say. The room was so quiet, she could hear the ticking from the clock up front.

Liza looked up to see the young volunteer seated behind the front table just like a test proctor for a final exam. She wasn't the source of the movement. It had to be a camera crew.

I must have really been off in sudoku land if I didn't hear the door open, Liza thought. The camera people had to be making great efforts to keep quiet. She resisted the instinctive response of turning to look at them—and the childish urge to hide her work from the glass and metal eye peeking over her shoulder. She just set her jaw and continued working.

Was Will sitting with Charley in another room, looking at the feed from this camera and doing professional commentary?

"See, Charley, she's wasting time tracing a useless swordfish when she could eliminate a whole slew of sixes with this swordfish over here."

Gritting her teeth still harder, Liza derailed that train of thought. No second-guessing. She continued on until she again lost herself in the flow of numbers.

She'd not heard the reappearance of the crew as she wrestled through several more swordfish, then reached the tipping point where more and more spaces got filled through simpler techniques. They were definitely behind her as she checked over her solution.

Of course, they'd want to be in close for the kill.

Okay. It worked out. Liza raised her hand, causing a bit of a stir among the other contestants. The volunteer came to take her puzzle and then nodded almost imperceptibly toward the door in the rear.

It took Liza a moment to take the hint. *Well, duh. Why should I sit around here? Especially when the camera people probably want to film my exit?*

Liza rose, trying not to make any noise and also avoiding eye contact with the camera. She went to the right-hand side of the pair of double doors, gently twisted the knob, pushed, and stepped through.

As the panel swung shut behind her, cutting off the camera's view, Liza released a long-held breath.

The corridor outside the event rooms stood empty except for a tournament volunteer acting as hall monitor. Of course, with the doors opening to admit camera crews, both Will and Charley wouldn't want any extraneous noise disturbing the contestants or the camera sound levels.

Liza heard a subdued murmur of voices coming from one end of the hallway. She followed the sound to the large open area in front of the Skye Room.

The doors to the ballroom were closed, but a good number of people had congregated in the anteroom—audience members who had stood in the rear for the original first round plus some of the contestants who'd given up. Liza recognized the potbellied guy Roche had interrogated after Ian Quirk collapsed.

Some people actually clapped as Liza arrived, and her cheering section quickly converged on her. "You're the first person to come out here," Kevin told her.

"Of course," Michael pointed out, "there's another way out from those rooms. That much we found out before they chased us away."

"A TV camera crew came by and filmed us," Mrs. Halvorsen said. "But then a young woman marched over and said we had to get out of there. We didn't want to be a distraction for you."

So somebody like Roy Conklin who hates crowds could just sneak off to the elevators and make a getaway with no fuss and no one the wiser, Liza thought. *On the other hand, I'd expect Babs Basset to come out here with a brass band to receive an ovation from her subjects.*

And speak of the devil, who swept in at that moment but Babs herself. She looked a little put out seeing Liza already there, but managed a gracious enough response to the smattering of applause she received.

"It seems they were considerably more organized last year," she shared with the room in general. "As soon as contestants submitted solutions, they were checked. So much more *certain*, especially for the—"

Liza was almost certain the next word would be something like "peasants" or "nobodies." But Babs came up with "first-time contestants" instead, although her tone made the other meanings crystal clear.

How nice—Babs worked in a double-barreled disparagement of the participants in the tournament and Will's running it, Liza thought, but she managed to keep her mouth shut.

Scottie Terhune appeared. Babs gave him a superior smile, but that curdled when he announced, "So this is where the party is! Guess I must have taken the long way around."

True or not, Liza enjoyed watching the uncertainty about Scottie's finishing time slip past Babs's armor.

Some other new faces filtered in, then Gemma Vereker entered to general applause.

"Really," Babs sniffed. "It's not as if she set any records."

But Gemma did finish in a respectable time, Liza thought, and more people were glad to see her.

Michael consulted his watch and leaned close. "It's seven-fifteen. Time's up."

The anteroom really began to fill as recently released contestants crowded in. Finally, Will Singleton made his way to the center of the growing mob scene. He pulled a sheet of paper from his portfolio.

"I'm pleased to announce that sixty contestants successfully solved the puzzle in the allotted time."

"So few," Babs murmured. Liza could have spit at this hypocritical concern for the "little people" Babs could care less about. "Doesn't dear Will realize that odds like that can only discourage the casual viewers?"

"It doesn't seem to hurt those poker programs," Scottie pointed out. "They usually only concentrate on the top ten out of maybe a thousand entrants."

"Poker." Babs made the game sound too déclassé for words.

"Last year, only the top five contestants in five elimination rounds advanced to the finals," Liza said. "That was probably the same proportion."

Babs didn't respond. In fact, she turned her back on Liza, all her attention on Will as he prepared to read out the names of the five top scorers.

Maybe it was the avid way Babs eyed Will and his

portfolio, but Liza had a sudden flashback—a glimpse of the portfolio lying on the podium during the publicity get-together . . . and Babs pulling her hand back. At the time, Liza thought maybe Ms. Basset had been trying for an advance peek at the competition puzzle. Considering how things turned out at SINN's Irvine headquarters, could she have gotten at the portfolio to mess up Will's promotional puzzle?

Will held up the sheet of paper. "In first place, Roy Conklin." That got a soft hiss from Babs. To tell the truth, Liza had a hard time not joining in.

"Next, Liza Kelly." That was better—although not for Babs.

"Third, Scottie Terhune." Babs's hiss turned into something more like a groan.

"Fourth, Barbara Basset." Babs didn't mind leading a brief spatter of applause.

"And in fifth place, Dr. H. Dunphy."

Babs straightened with a strangled, *"What?"*

At the same moment, a muscular guy popped out of the crowd, a malicious smile on his chiseled features. "Hey, Babs. Long time no see."

Liza wished she knew this guy's secret. For the first time since she'd met Babs, the woman stood speechless.

Michael took advantage of the silence to get a few words in. "The restaurant where this big hoedown is supposed to take place tonight is called Angus, so I guess we can expect some good steaks."

Fergus Fleming appeared behind them. "That's an American thing, to connect the name 'Angus' to beef," he said. "Angus is the name of the ancient Celtic god of love. It's also the name of our chef. And while you can indeed get a good steak at our restaurant, tonight we're offering a traditional Scots feast." He gestured expansively, his teeth showing white against his red beard. "We're piping in the haggis!"

Liza hoped she had a good smile in place, because whenever she heard of something being "piped in," she had a memory from her childhood days. Spending summers wandering all over Maiden's Bay, she and her friends had discovered a giant pipe at one end of the beach. And when the tide receded to reveal an opening large enough to swallow them, they also discovered the stink of the area's sewage being pumped out.

"Sounds like an adventure," Liza said in a faint voice.

"Not for me." Babs had gotten her voice back, and it was venomous. "They may have forced me to accept that man's hospitality, but I will never share a meal with him."

"What's your trouble with Mr. Fleming?" Liza asked.

Babs continued to follow the big Scotsman with her eyes, her look getting more baleful as he stopped for an animated chat with Gemma Vereker and Will. "Oh, he may have a sort of surface Celtic charm, but that can lead to real trouble, believe me."

"How?"

"You could end up married to him," Babs snapped. Then it was Liza's turn to stand speechless as Babs Basset stormed off.

8

As soon as Babs was out of earshot, Liza began herding her friends in the opposite direction. "Come on. I want to go over some of that stuff Michelle sent us."

Back upstairs in the suite, Liza went immediately to her laptop, calling up the data on Babs Basset. "What do you know? Hubby number three was Fergus Fleming."

"Well, I missed that," Michael admitted.

"Who would have been looking for it?" Mrs. Halvorsen wanted to know.

Liza got the phone. "I think that's something Buck ought to know."

When she got hold of him, though, she discovered he already knew. "I caught the name and looked into it. Seems Babs met Fleming while he was managing a hotel in Europe and married him. I guess she fancied herself a latter-day Ivana Trump. It didn't last, though. And thanks to a sloppy prenup, Fleming actually came out of the divorce with a chunk of Babs's change."

"Which he apparently invested in Rancho Pacificano," Liza said. "I remember him being introduced as the managing partner."

"You got it," Buck confirmed.

"Wow, no wonder Babs kept giving him dirty looks—especially when Fleming was with Gemma Vereker."

Liza thought for a moment. "There's another thing. A little while before that disaster of a publicity stunt, Will left his portfolio lying unattended—the portfolio holding all his puzzles. And I saw Babs standing nearby—moving away actually."

"You think she might have been looking inside?" Buck asked.

"I think she was screwing around with the puzzle that was going to be on television," Liza replied. "She's out to sabotage Will's standing with SINN." She paused again. "And she may be striking at Fergus Fleming, too. He agreed to host the tournament because he figured it would be a showcase for Rancho Pacificano on nationwide television. Professionally speaking, it's not the greatest publicity in the world to have a guest drop dead."

"I dunno." Buck sounded dubious. "If Fergus was the one who dropped dead, I could see more of a connection—more of a motive."

"There's something else I saw that was a little weird," Liza went on. "When Will read off the list of the five top-scoring contestants, Babs sort of went into shock when she heard the last name—Dr. H. Dunphy. And then this guy approached her and said, 'Long time no see.'"

Notebook pages flapped on the other end of the connection. "That's not the name of any of the other previous husbands. Could he be an old boyfriend, maybe? Or someone else she screwed over?" Buck thought for a moment. "Maybe you'd be better off getting a line on him."

"I'll ask around this evening at the big dinner," Liza promised. And with that decided, they ended the call.

"Ready to go?" she asked Michael.

"I was going to ask the same thing of these two," he said with a smile. "Have you got someplace exciting you're going to go zooming off to?"

"Not exactly zooming," Mrs. H. reported, sounding a little disappointed. "We're taking a taxi."

"Some technical problems with the car," Kevin said gruffly.

"You should have mentioned it earlier. I could have lent you the Honda." Michael managed to rub salt in the wound even while sounding generous.

Liza grabbed his arm. "I think we'd better get moving." As soon as they were out the door, she added, "After all, a moving target is harder to hit."

Michael raised his hands. "All right, all right. I'll be a good boy while you investigate."

When they arrived down at Angus, Liza wasn't sure she'd get in any investigating at all. She could hear the loud chattering well before they even got to the entrance of the closed restaurant. The maitre d' stood barring the way until Liza passed over her invitation. Then she realized that according to the fancy printing on the heavy stock, they were already well into the cocktail hour.

Not that there were many cocktails in evidence. Spread along the bar she saw a row of bottles, all high-end single malt Scotch. Michael had a Macallan, neat. Liza determinedly ordered a ginger ale. "The last time I had a bit too much to drink, I wound up finding a dead body and entertaining the cops dressed only in a towel—and not much of a towel," she muttered.

Michael sipped his whiskey. "From what I hear, they were very entertained." He took a long breath. "Smooth, but potent. I'm not sure if this is for social lubrication, or to help get the Scottish cuisine down."

Fergus Fleming appeared in the Highland version of black tie, wearing a short, black velvet jacket and a kilt in red, black, and yellow. "I'm a MacAlister on my mother's side, so I'm allowed to wear the tartan," he said, offering a professional glad hand. "You had us worried—we've had a few no-shows."

"Ms. Basset," Liza said.

Fleming's lips compressed as he nodded. "And Mr.

Conklin—apparently he doesn't do well with large, lively groups, which we hope this will be. You'll join me at the head table, along with Ms. Vereker and Mr. Singleton. After dinner, he'll talk about where sudoku came from, where it's going—"

He broke off with a quizzical glance at the drink in Liza's hand. "Not traditional."

"It is for Liza's line of work." Gemma Vereker appeared. "She's expected to keep her head while her clients lush it up."

From their similar florid complexions, she must have been matching him drink for drink.

After a little more chitchat, Liza went off in search of Will Singleton. She found him with a glass of whiskey in his hand, too.

"So, Will, do you want to tell me about this Dr. Dunphy guy?"

"You didn't hear that story? I thought it was all over the sudoku world."

"Contrary to rumor, Will, I don't have spies everywhere."

Will shrugged and gave her an owlish look. "Dr. Humphrey Dunphy taught economics and was the go-to guy on sudoku for the San Francisco media. He knew his stuff, but he talked like a college professor—and he was heavy."

"But now Babs Basset is the Frisco queen of sudoku," Liza said.

"Yeah." Will took another sip. "First came the whispering campaign and a nickname—Humphrey Dumpy. Then Babs started insinuating herself with the local stations. And . . . you know. Whatever you think of her personality, she looks great on the screen."

"She pushed him out of the spotlight," Liza said. *Just as she's trying to do to you, Will.*

He shrugged. "Dunphy left town. Apparently he relocated to Phoenix and created a second act for himself. He lost weight, and now he's back to compete in the tournament." Will's enunciation wasn't as clear as it could be.

Liza figured he'd better have a good meal before he got up to speak.

Still, she couldn't get the image of Babs and the portfolio out of her head. "You know, Will, I was thinking about that puzzle you gave to Charley—and how it would only take a second for someone to alter it."

Will blinked. "In my portfolio?"

"You didn't hold on to it every instant. Do you still have the puzzle? More important, do you still have it on your computer? Maybe you should print out a new copy for comparison."

"Maybe," he said vaguely. Liza had the sinking feeling Will wouldn't even remember this conversation.

Instead, he surprised her. "That's what I really appreciate about you, Liza. You're always concerned. It's like when you write about Sudoku Nation in your columns. You believe it should be a democracy. Babs . . ." He made a face. "She wants to be the queen, calling the shots. Quirk thought he would be the philosopher king, laying down the law. I suppose I'm like that, too, except I try to get people involved. Young Terhune . . . he was just glad to find something involving numbers that he was good at. Still, he got his old company to hold a yearly sudoku get-together for kids."

He frowned. "That won't be happening anymore. And Roy Conklin, he uses it to show students that they don't have to be afraid of numbers. The thing is, none of them— and that includes me—is able to do what you do. I don't know if you can win this tournament. I didn't mention it when I announced the leaders, but you're only seconds apart. All I'll say is, it will be a damn shame if you don't."

Liza couldn't imagine an answer to that, so she didn't give one. "I think it would be a shame if someone was trying to ruin this tournament—for any reason. Promise me you'll print out a copy of the puzzle?"

Will promised and moved on. A second later, Fergus Fleming moved to the center of the room and boomed out, "Ladies and gentlemen, please find your seats. If you don't know where they are, consult with Mr. Roche."

Oliver Roche came over to join him—yes, clipboard in hand. Liza and Michael had little trouble finding the head table, where Fleming, Gemma, Will, and Scottie Terhune all sat, fortifying themselves with another round of drinks.

As she and Michael took their seats, Liza heard Gemma say, "I think I've taken on enough liquid courage to ask you, Fergus. Exactly what is this haggis we're supposed to be eating?"

"Ah," he said, though it came out more like "Och." Apparently Scotch whiskey made Fleming's Scots burr more prominent. "I think the poet Burns gave the best description when he called the haggis 'proud chieftain of the sausage race.'"

That information came as something of a relief for Liza. Ever since she'd heard Fleming talk about piping the stuff in, she'd had visions of some sort of sludgy brown soup.

"Sausage, huh?" Scottie said. "That can cover a variety of sins."

"They call you 'Scottie,' and you have no idea what goes into a haggis?" Fleming demanded.

"The 'Scottie' is a nickname," he answered. "And Terhune is a fine old Dutch name, with a side order of French. Besides, my family has been here so long, our national sausage is the hot dog."

"Well, I'll just put it this way," Fleming finally said. "We Scots are a thrifty people, and there's a good deal of meat left on a sheep after you take the lamb chops."

"What did they call those leftovers?" Michael said with a smile. "The lights and livers?"

"Probably some of that, along with other bits and pieces," Fleming agreed. "Chopped up, mixed with oatmeal, onions, and spices, wrapped in a sheep's stomach and boiled for three hours."

He took in the expressions on the other people at the table. "Och, you Americans," he said. "It's nothing ye havenae had in a hot dog, only not as finely ground."

Then Fleming glanced at the door and must have gotten

some sort of signal. He rose from his seat. "Be upstanding, please."

"I guess that's Scots for 'everybody up,'" Michael whispered to Liza.

"Welcome, everyone, to what I hope will be a memorable evening. Before we introduce the guest of honor, I ask Pastor Gordon to say a few words."

A man in a black suit and a clerical collar stood up at a nearby table. "I shall give the Selkirk Grace," he said, his Scots accent a bit fainter than Fleming's.

> "Some hae meat and canna eat,
> And some wad eat that want it,
> But we hae meat and we can eat,
> And sae the Lord be thankit."

That earned a round of applause from the well-oiled crowd, and servers brought out the first course, a cream of leek soup.

"Looks like Angus knows his stuff when it comes to soups," Michael whispered to Liza.

Fleming stood again, this time raising his glass of whiskey. "To your feet, please, ladies and gentlemen. I give you . . . the haggis!"

The entrance doors to the ballroom flew open, and silhouetted in the doorway stood a kilted figure that looked about seven feet tall. Then a wild blast of sound hit them—a skirling bagpipe march.

Oh, Liza thought, *that kind of piping.*

Michael brought his lips close to her ear. "I think Shakespeare has a line about people having a hard time holding their water when they hear the pipes. With all the drinking going on here, that could be a disaster."

As the piper advanced and the sound got louder, Liza remembered a cartoon she'd seen years ago. At first glance it looked like three bagpipers playing. Closer examination showed one of them had a cat, not a bagpipe, tucked under his arm—with the animal's tail between his teeth.

She finally realized that the bagpiper was only the leader in a brief procession. Behind him marched a short, stocky man in kitchen whites—Angus the chef, not the beef, Liza realized. Angus carried a silver tray raised high, and in the middle of the platter gleamed something that looked like a cross between a small football and a brown water balloon.

Fergus Fleming had begun clapping in time to the music, and the other guests followed suit. Then Liza realized there was a third member of the procession, a uniformed member of the staff cradling a large bottle of Scotch.

The little parade reached the head table, and Fleming called out, "Oliver, would you do the honors?"

Roche appeared, looking about as comfortable as a vegetarian at a hot dog–eating contest. He took a knife from Angus and proceeded to make a lengthwise incision on the displayed haggis.

"Good man!" Fleming said as everyone applauded. He relieved the third man of his bottle and leaned over the open haggis. "Perhaps a wee bit of whiskey sauce!" Fergus cried, splashing a little Scotch onto the steaming contents.

"Well, that ought to sterilize everything," Michael whispered.

More clapping followed as the piper played a new tune, leading the march to the kitchen.

Soon enough, the servers reappeared bearing large plates. "What goes with the haggis?" Liza asked, trying to get a look.

"Champit neeps and tatties," Fleming replied. "That's mashed turnips and—"

"Potatoes?" Liza guessed.

"Spot on!" Fergus complimented her.

By then, the plates had actually arrived. Half the plate was taken up with a chunky brownish mound, the rest with a whitish mound and a yellowish mound.

I guess in this case, tradition trumps presentation, Liza thought, looking down in silence.

She poked a tentative fork at the mass of haggis.

"Stout hearts, now," Fleming encouraged. "It is good, I promise you."

"Well, the rest of me didn't get stout by turning down a meal," Scottie said. "I went to a school that served the world's worst meals. By way of protest, I'd eat the Styrofoam plates, too."

Fleming offered a cut-glass bowl. "Some folk prefer a wee bit of horseradish," he suggested.

Scottie took a forkful of the condiment, dropped it atop the haggis, and then scooped a good amount of the mixture into his mouth.

Beaming, Fergus did the same—but he quickly stopped chewing with a frown. Scottie took another serving, then coughed.

"No, lad." Fleming made a "hands down" gesture to Scottie and the others at the table, who were still nerving themselves for a mouthful. "I'm embarrassed to say—"

Another cough from Scottie interrupted him.

Liza turned to her fellow sudokologist. Scottie looked even redder than the whiskey he'd consumed would warrant.

Could that be the horseradish? Liza thought.

Scottie's face seemed not just red, but swollen. The whites of his eyes had gone a bright pink, too. He tried to say something but couldn't.

All he managed to do was tap his wrist as he fell from his seat.

9

Silence fell over the restaurant, then a buzz of questions as people began getting to their feet, trying to see what had happened.

Oliver Roche appeared in a broken-field run through the gawkers. "What's going on?" he demanded a little breathlessly.

"Scottie fell," Liza said. "I think he's choking." She was already on her knees, loosening his tie and shirt. "It's like his throat is swelling."

"Did he say anything?" Roche knelt beside her, almost in a replay of what he'd done when Ian Quirk collapsed.

"No, but he was tapping his left wrist."

Roche pulled back Scottie's cuff to reveal a metal bracelet. "This says he's got a shellfish allergy." He immediately pulled out a cell phone to dial 911.

"But—but there's no shellfish in haggis." Fergus Fleming's boozy bonhomie had vanished, Scotch fumes boiled off as he was shocked closer to sobriety. His accent disappeared, as well.

The hotelier stared down at his plate, his eyes clearing a little more. "But then, this haggis tastes funny."

Fleming shot to his feet, looked around, and saw everyone else in the place eating—or trying to eat—the haggis. "Everyone!" he said in his loudest voice, raising his arms. "I regret to interrupt your dinner, but you'll have to . . . interrupt your dinner. No. Please stop. I'm afraid there's a—er . . ." He fumbled for words, painting a ghastly smile on his face. "There's a wee problem with the haggis."

A look of sudden panic wiped out that smile. "There's no one else—I mean, no one here with any fish allergy, is there?"

The Scottish clergyman who'd done the grace looked puzzled. "But there's no seafood in haggis."

"Aye," Fergus said, "that's the wee problem."

The paramedics arrived all prepared this time, ready to deal with anaphylactic shock. They gave Scottie an injection, but Liza could see that his face had gone from congested to waxy pale.

As the ambulance people wheeled their gurney away, Liza had another burst of déjà vu. The crew had that same grim, hopeless look on their faces.

This time, Detective Janacek didn't need convincing to come out to Rancho Pacificano. He arrived on the double with a complete crime-scene team, confiscating the diners' meals and sealing off the kitchen.

Angus the chef appeared to protest this invasion of his domain. But if the stocky chef was aggravated before, he nearly burst a blood vessel at the idea of shellfish getting into his haggis.

"It isnae possible!" he hissed, his own Scots accent peeking out in his agitation.

"You don't have any fish in your kitchen?" Janacek asked.

"Of course we have fish—trout, salmon, and haddock. We smoke it for the finnan haddie and cullen skink," Angus replied. "But there was none of it out yesterday. We were closed all day, preparing the haggis."

"Well, unless this Terhune fellow also had an allergy to oatmeal, something went wrong in your kitchen." The detective's broad face looked hard but also worried. Obviously, two possible murders in the same place on the same day stretched coincidence a little too fine for Pete Janacek's liking.

Liza walked down the hallway to the Hebrides Room, heading for a more intimate function than the others she'd been to. No cocktails and canapés or sudoku contests, but at least no one had died there.

She'd been invited to give a statement, an event about as optional as one of Michelle Markson's demands. Sure, she could say no, enjoy a lovely ride to police headquarters in the back of a squad car, and still be questioned, just under less pleasant circumstances.

Well, it was only a statement, after all. She saw no need to get on the phone to Michelle and have her unleash Alvin Hunzinger, Lawyer to the Stars. The guy might look like Elmer Fudd, but Liza had seen him reduce competent police detectives to piles of steaming frustration.

"Get in, take care of the formalities, and get out," Liza told herself as she reached for the doorknob. Before she could actually grasp the darned thing, it pulled away from her fingertips as the door was yanked open.

A tall, young detective who looked sort of like Sherlock Holmes except for the May suit stood in the opening. Liza recognized him as the guy who'd been sacrificed to keep Oliver Roche away from the rest of the investigators that afternoon.

From the look on his sharp features, the experience may have soured him—or maybe he'd been recruited to play bad cop in the forthcoming interview.

He stepped out of the way, silent but polite enough, and

gestured Liza into the room. The chairs and tables hadn't
been cleared away after this evening's competition round,
but then they'd probably be needed in the same places for
tomorrow.

Janacek had established himself behind the monitor's
table at the far end of the room with a couple of competitors' seats from the first row pulled up to face him.

The detective consulted his notebook, reading "Liza
Kelly" aloud. As if he needed that prop. Pete Janacek
might be broad in the face and in the beam, but Liza had
dealt with enough police types to look at the eyes. And
Janacek had eyes that missed nothing.

"Good evening, Detectives," she said, taking one of the
seats. Young Holmes didn't sit. Instead, he stood somewhere behind her. Was that supposed to put her on edge?
Liza decided to ignore him and put her full attention on the
older member of the partnership.

"I'd like you to tell me everything that happened at the
table before Mr. Terhune collapsed." Janacek didn't seem
to be going for Mr. Good Cop. He kept his voice neutral,
very "Just the facts, ma'am."

Liza described all the ritual byplay, piping in the haggis, the Selkirk Grace, and then the conversation about
Scottish cuisine leading up to Scottie's disastrous attempt
at chowing down the unappetizing delicacy.

"So none of you had eaten haggis before?" Janacek
asked.

"Except for Mr. Fleming, of course," Liza replied. "Nobody else mentioned it. I have to admit I wasn't quite sure
what haggis was until Fergus explained."

Young Holmes suddenly spoke up. "Mr. Terhune was
sitting right beside you at dinner. And Mr. Quirk had been
seated right behind you at the competition."

Liza shot him a look over her shoulder. "Yes, if someone
saw me shoving peanuts down one guy's mouth and oysters
down the other's, this whole thing would be solved."

She turned her attention back to Janacek. "I had something strange happen to me this afternoon. A friend took

me for a ride in the hills, and the car suddenly went crazy."

Janacek leaned forward. "What exactly happened?"

Liza explained about the car's strange shimmying. "It put us in the wrong lane several times. If another car had been coming our way . . ."

"You didn't report this to the police, though?" Young Holmes interrupted.

"I have to admit, I was more concerned about getting back here for the competition," Liza confessed. "Until Scottie keeled over at the table, I hadn't really thought about it. Now I'd have to wonder if someone is going after the better-known sudoku people at the tournament."

The older detective pursed his lips and stared at her in silence as the moment stretched out. But if Janacek thought this was going to crack a veteran of the Michelle Markson wars, he was way too optimistic.

Finally, Janacek spoke. "My friend Mr. Roche told me that you had a certain reputation in the media for solving crimes, that you'd gotten a lot of publicity—"

"You think I was hoping to get famous from any of those? I had friends in trouble—or worse."

"And what friend was in trouble today when Mr. Roche reported you bringing a private investigator onto the property?" Janacek asked.

"Will Singleton is a friend who put a lot of work into setting up this tournament," Liza shot back angrily. "And Scottie Terhune . . . I hope he comes through. He's a friend, too."

She took a deep breath. "There's a lot more going on here than puzzles. Will managed a nationwide TV reach with SINN, but both Babs Basset and Quirk were trying to cut him out."

"That doesn't seem to have worked out for Mr. Quirk." Was that a snide tone creeping into the young detective's voice?

"But it worked once for Babs with a local rival," Liza shot back. "She drove him right out of San Francisco—and she wasn't pleased to find that he'd turned up here for the weekend."

She decided not to mention Scottie and his financial motive—not with him hovering between life and death.

Janacek's cell phone rang and he opened it. "Yes, Doctor . . . ah."

It sounded as if Scottie wasn't hovering anymore.

Clicking his phone shut, Janacek said, "I'm very sorry to tell you that your friend—"

Liza squeezed her eyes shut, afraid tears would start leaking out. "Why would anyone do this to Scottie? He could be a bit much sometimes, but I don't think he had an enemy in the world."

"Perhaps, but you've raised some other interesting questions," the detective said.

Liza took a deep breath.

"I haven't even raised the bad blood between Babs and Mr. Fleming—they were married," she said.

"You seem to have a great interest in Ms. Basset. But at the time of this incident, she was in Ms. Ormond's room for a business dinner—room service. And for your information, Professor Conklin was in his room, preparing a lecture for tomorrow morning. Room service delivered an order of sandwiches just as the main course was being served downstairs."

"So they obviously weren't around when Scottie ate whatever disagreed with him." Liza frowned. "On the other hand, Fergus Fleming told us the haggis had to boil in those bags for three hours. Do you think it was under somebody's watchful eye the whole time?"

Janacek made some marks in his notebook. "Something else to ask that Angus character." He gave Liza a look— not exactly threatening, but not friendly, either. "It would seem we're done for the time being, Ms. Kelly. I hope you won't be going far."

Liza's stomach complained—loudly. "Just far enough to get something to eat," she told the detective. "I hear the restaurant here is closed for the night."

Michael stood waiting for her outside in the hallway. "One of Janacek's underlings took a quick statement," he said. "I began to wonder if you were in for the third degree."

"Not arrested, just hungry," Liza told him.

"I was thinking the same thing." Michael led her outside to the lot where his car was parked. "You know, the next town over is Costa Mesa . . ."

"That taco place!" Liza exclaimed.

"One of the hidden jewels of Orange County," Michael said with a smile. "It's still there, you know—I passed the joint while I was driving around, looking for a place to stay."

It had been years since Liza had been to the taqueria. It had been in the early days of their marriage, when they had to stretch every nickel, that a friend of Michael's had put him on to the place. Great food, inexpensive prices, and a fair-sized drive from Westwood, it had made for a nice, budget-conscious day trip.

As finances became better, the taco pilgrimage had become a sentimental journey, and then . . . then they never had time for it anymore. Well, Liza hadn't. She'd become ever more embroiled with her partnership at Markson Associates. And then Michael had left and Liza had been forced to reassess priorities.

"Hey," Michael said, interrupting her rueful musings, "We're here." He turned the old Honda through a driveway and into a parking lot, and Liza smiled. The taco place looked as if it had never changed. It was a typical brick roadside stand, painted orange and royal blue. A faded awning stretched over an outdoor seating area.

They went inside to the odors of grilling meat, spices— and yes, a bit of grease. Liza's stomach made its interest known with some embarrassingly loud noises.

"Hush," Liza quietly told it. "You'll get something soon."

They ordered three burritos, chicken for her, carne asada for him, and a black bean to share.

"It's nice enough out. What do you say we sit in the open?" Michael suggested.

The folding chairs had slatted seats, just as she remembered—and about as comfortable as she remembered, too. But then, the genius of this place lay in the food, not the dining experience.

Getting the large, overstuffed soft taco to her mouth was a two-handed job. Each burrito was really a meal in itself—seasoned meat, shredded lettuce, chunked tomato, cheese, salsa, guacamole—all of the ingredients ready to burst forth and trickle down her chin. Liza always joked that eating here had been her earliest training in publicity. You needed the highest level of confidence to deal with those huge burritos without disaster.

She forced herself to take human bites and not wolf her food down. Finally, she sat back, replete, taking a sip of soda and trying not to burp too loudly.

"You know in some parts of the world, that's an indication of appreciation for a meal," Michael told her.

"Yeah, well, we don't have any Arabian sheikhs for clients—or Chinese industrialists," Liza replied, stifling another outburst. She shifted uncomfortably on her seat. "What next?"

Michael rose from the little table, gathering up their trash for deposit. "I thought we could go for a little drive."

"Not into the hills, please. I had enough excitement there for one day."

Michael's eyes sharpened as they headed for the car. "What happened? Kevin mentioned technical difficulties."

While getting in and snapping her seat belt in place, Liza told him the story of their record-setting skid.

"So we've got two sudoku whizzes poisoned and one nearly crunched." Michael leaned through the open car window toward her. Liza noticed that in spite of the barber's best efforts to neaten things, Michael's hair had gotten tousled again, his curls reasserting themselves. It made for a strange juxtaposition with the grim expression on his face. "I don't suppose you could suddenly find urgent business in someplace like Outer Mongolia, could you?"

"What?" She stared at him. "Give up the tournament, run out on Will, disappoint Mrs. H.—"

"And probably break Kevin's heart," Michael finished for her in a treacly voice.

In more normal tones, he went on, ignoring her dirty look. "Face it, Liza. This isn't exactly a normal sudoku tournament. The odds-on favorite hits the floor before he finishes the first puzzle. The number two seed—that's you—has interesting car trouble. And number three gets very sick at supper—"

"He's dead," Liza interrupted. "Detective Janacek got the call before he dismissed me."

Michael strode round to his side of the car, got in, and leaned across the seat toward her. "This. Is. Not. Good." He spaced out each word for emphasis. "I thought maybe this was just hardball sudoku, stuff to throw off the competition. I mean, Quirk could have—should have—noticed the smell of peanuts in the air much earlier. Terhune inhaled too much of that haggis, trying to prove he wasn't afraid of anything that came on a plate. If he'd just nibbled at it—"

"He wouldn't have gotten as big a dose," Liza said. "He might just have gotten sick."

She grappled with the idea. "So you're saying that what happened might have been aimed at throwing people off their game. Quirk wouldn't have been able to finish the qualifying round. I was supposed to be too shaken to do well in the makeup. And Scottie would be under the weather for tomorrow's rounds."

But Michael objected to his own theory. "The problem is, somebody got killed during the first attempt. You'd think most people would pull back after that."

"Most sane people," Liza agreed. "Unless—maybe it was too late? Maybe the haggis and the car had already been tampered with?"

"There's always such a thing as an anonymous warning,"

Michael said. "To go ahead with such a plan—or even let it go ahead—suggests a stronger motive than we've figured out so far."

"Or a double motive—and a psychopath," Liza suggested.

"And I suppose you have a candidate in mind?"

She nodded. "Babs Basset. She wants to run the West Coast sudoku world and get a connection with SINN. That means she has to discredit Will Singleton by destroying his tournament. That would explain not only going after the contestants, but sabotaging the big promotional puzzle when it was unveiled."

Liza took a deep breath. "And then you have two guests getting sick—or dying—at a very public event at Rancho Pacificano, the resort Babs's former husband bought into with money from their divorce settlement. We've seen how crazy she gets, seeing him running things. And from the way she screwed over that Dunphy guy, we know she has absolutely no conscience when it comes to getting her own way."

"I'm surprised you aren't dragging up that other old chestnut," Michael said. "You know, how poison is a woman's weapon?"

The word left Liza fighting a shudder, suddenly remembering Fleming's panicked inquiry tonight at dinner. What if someone else in the restaurant tonight had a fish allergy? What if they had a peanut allergy and were sitting near Quirk?

"On the other hand, I can't imagine someone with Babs's Lady of the Manor act fooling around with Kevin's car," Michael pointed out. "That would require an accomplice."

"Somebody who didn't—or hasn't yet—connected that dirty trick with the poisonings," Liza suggested.

Michael only shook his head at that one. "I think you have a lot more work to do on that theory. Also, I think you'll have to wait, because I don't like to argue when I drive—too distracting."

Especially if somebody tried something with this car, Liza thought mutinously.

Michael made his way south to the Pacific Coast Highway, crossing onto the Balboa Peninsula. "You remember the next step on our traditional agenda?"

"The Balboa Fun Zone," Liza replied. Up ahead rose the neon-decorated Ferris wheel—a local landmark. In the old days, rides on the wheel and the merry-go-round were mandatory. Liza had always been fascinated when reaching the top of the arc on the Ferris wheel. Depending on which way you looked, you had a view of the lights of Newport on one side and the darkness of the Pacific on the other.

Tonight, though . . . she put a hand on Michael's shoulder.

"I understand," he said quietly. "Even though it's Friday, for you it's a school night."

"I wish we could spend more time . . ." She wasn't sure whether she meant time away from the pressure cooker of the tournament or time with Michael, picking up threads of their past.

"Well, we can still make the circuit of the bay," Michael said, driving past the amusement area and pulling over to the landing for the Balboa Ferry. It wasn't a big line, but then, these weren't big boats. Each ferry only accommodated three cars.

Soon, though, they were aboard for the five-minute run to Balboa Island. Then it would just be a case of traversing the island, crossing the bridge to the mainland, and heading north to the Rancho Pacificano property. And then?

"Penny for your thoughts," Michael said.

"I'm glad we're riding with a navigator," Liza said. "Because as things stand right now, I'm not sure where the heck we are."

10

They drove off the ferry, completing the circuit around Newport Bay pretty much in silence. As Michael turned onto the drive leading to Rancho Pacificano, Liza managed a smile.

"I sort of feel as though I should tell you what a lovely evening I had," she said.

Michael smiled back as he pulled up at the main building. "I guess that's a bit difficult, considering the way this evening started."

"So do you mind if I just say that parts were really good?" Liza asked.

Michael leaned forward, and they kissed—for a while. He sighed, but Liza moved his hands away as they wound around her. "Let's not start something we can't finish," she warned.

"Yeah." His smile got a little lopsided, but it was still a smile. "I guess we don't want to shock poor Mrs. Halvorsen. And it's way past bedtime for most of the kids where I'm staying."

They kissed again, with a bit more restraint this time. Liza got out of the car, and Michael drove off to his motel.

Heading across the lobby, Liza had just one thing in mind—well, more like a succession of things: getting to her room, brushing her teeth, heading for bed . . .

"Excuse me—Ms. Kelly?" the young man behind the front desk called to her.

"How did you know—?" Liza began.

The young reception guy just shrugged. "Whenever there's a major event, we get pictures of the special guests. Ms. Vereker left this for you." He held out an envelope—the hotel stationery, Liza realized.

She tore off one end and extracted the note from inside.

Liza, she read.

The nice fellow at the front desk promised faithfully that one of the staff will give me a wake-up call at nine o'clock, but . . .

Could you please knock on my door here in Room 315 about a half an hour later to make sure I'm actually on my feet and taking notice? I can manage the discipline to be up before it's bright and early for a movie shoot, but when it's for a sudoku puzzle at noon . . . well, I could use the help.

Thanks,
G.

Liza folded the note and put it in her pocket with a shrug. "Just another part of the all-inclusive services from Markson Associates," she told herself as she headed up to her own room and her own bed.

The next morning, Liza was up well before nine, getting herself ready for the day. Mrs. Halvorsen's door stood slightly open, and Liza had a brief qualm about disturbing her neighbor.

Well, there's no tie hanging from it, so there shouldn't be anything too embarrassing, she silently told herself as she approached. When she heard the regular breathing of deep sleep, she stepped softly away. This was supposed to be a bit of a vacation for Mrs. H. Liza decided to let her enjoy herself. Why wake her up just because Liza didn't want to find herself running around like a nut right before the next round of competition?

And something that had struck her while she brushed her teeth suggested that some running around might be in order.

If the cops have closed the kitchen, we may have a bit of a problem getting breakfast around here, Liza thought as she tied the laces on her Saucony running shoes. *Like it or not, we'll be stuck on the Detective Janacek Diet.*

In fact, Liza debated calling Michael to collect an order from Denny's or maybe some breakfast tacos from last night's restaurant as she headed down the hallway to Gemma Vereker's room.

She knocked on the door and got some sort of noise in response. Then the door opened, and a half-dressed and slightly worse for wear Gemma welcomed her. "Sorry, Liza. I'm afraid I've been acting too much like a movie star lately. Usually, I don't need minders, but I'd appreciate it if you would check in, especially if I'm still in the running tomorrow morning. I'd hate to get myself disqualified by oversleeping."

Grinning, Liza nodded. "I guess it's easy enough to act like a movie star with all that expensive Scotch floating around last night."

Gemma winced. "Not to mention the somewhat cheaper champagne a bit earlier. Let me put on my face and a top, and then we'll explore the breakfast situation."

The actress went into the bathroom, and Liza stood waiting in the suite's sitting room. She smiled as she spotted a magazine with a sudoku puzzle sticking out from under Gemma's purse. *Always practicing, eh?*

Deciding to get a look at Gemma's solving techniques,

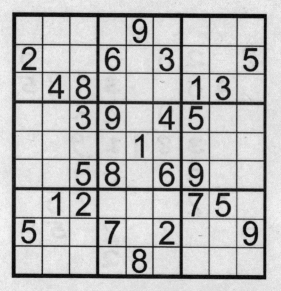

Liza teased the paper out. It was from an airline in-flight magazine, and it was not exactly the most difficult sudoku Liza had ever seen.

That's why Liza frowned as she looked over Gemma's attempted solution. Not one of the digits Gemma had inked in was in the right place, and it didn't take much to see that. Often, a neighboring number and sometimes two invalidated Gemma's choices.

If this was the level of competence Gemma displayed, how had she done so well solving Will's puzzles? Either she was pretty crocked on the flight from New York, or . . .

Liza shook her head. No. The Will Singleton she knew would never play with puzzle results to keep a celebrity in the tournament.

"There, done," Gemma called.

Liza hastily moved away from the table as Gemma

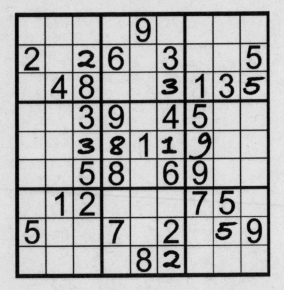

emerged, fully dressed and made up. The actress scooped up her bag, stashing the butchered puzzle inside. "I'll admit that things got a bit hazy toward the end of the evening," she said, "but I seem to remember Fergus Fleming promising something for this morning."

That something turned out to be an improvised breakfast buffet in the hotel lobby. Angus and his people had indeed been exiled from the kitchen, but the chef had rounded up some chafing dishes and supplies and was making like a short-order cook, doing up eggs and omelets while his cohorts grilled ham, bacon, and sausages. They'd also set up tables with cereal, chilled pitchers of milk, urns for coffee, decaf, and tea, platters of sliced fruit, and display baskets filled to overflowing with rolls and pastries.

"Excellent," Gemma said, surveying the bounty. "I'll have one of each."

They didn't—quite—but both of them had well-laden

plates as they stepped outside to find a table for two on the tree-shaded patio.

Liza looked about at the plants surrounding them. "These aren't going to bother you, are they?"

Gemma took a deep breath, let it out, and shrugged. "Guess not. The problem is, I can never tell. I did a Western some years ago, filming on location somewhere in West Cupcake, and something in the air just shut me down. They got a lot of footage of me walking and riding around this town, but I had to do all of my dialogue on a sound stage back in L.A. I could barely breathe out there, much less talk."

She took another deep breath. "If there was anything here that would start this up, I'd be wheezing already." She laughed. "I remember my manager Artie bought some sort of dried plant to brighten up his office. Next time I went to visit him, I could barely breathe." Gemma gave Liza a crooked smile. "I told him that if he expected to keep me away with that damned thing, it would work better than he hoped—I'd find myself a new manager."

They'd just settled down to eat when Will Singleton came rushing by as if the hounds of hell were after him. He all but screeched to a halt when he saw Liza. "I did what you suggested last night." Will rummaged in his portfolio. "Look here."

Liza looked at the sheet he extended and instantly recognized the puzzle.

"This is how it printed out." Will's voice was tight.

Gemma craned her neck, trying to get a look. "What is it?" she asked.

"It's the puzzle for the promo event at SINN headquarters," Liza explained. "But here one of the extra eights—"

"I'd call it more embarrassing than extra," Will grumbled.

"One of the numbers that fouled things up turns out to be a three," Liza went on.

"That's how it was in the computer, but not how it was on the fax to SINN," Will said. "So this morning I sat down

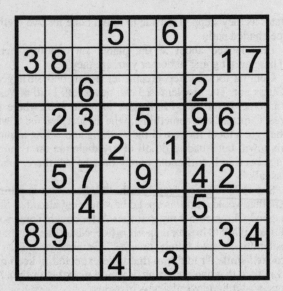

with a magnifying glass. The original I gave to Charley Ormond was definitely altered. When you look carefully, the ink on that second eight is different."

"Well, then, I think you should take them both to Charley and show her." Liza frowned as she took in the agitated expression on Will's face. "Look, you've got proof," Liza began.

"Proof that convinces me, and I guess you," Will said unhappily. "But would it convince someone who doesn't know me?"

He turned to Gemma, who responded with a long, drawn-out "Ahhhhhhhhhh . . ."

Will nodded violently. "Exactly. I don't know if waving printouts at Charley will convince her. She might just think I was trying to cover my ass after a monumental screwup."

His agitation intensified. "Or worse, she might believe me . . . and decide I've lost all control of this tournament.

What if the person who's responsible for all these disasters is another invitee? Charley—and SINN—could easily say it was all my fault."

Liza opened her mouth to reply, but nothing came out. Will had very neatly hooked himself on the horns of a damnably difficult dilemma. Neither hunkering down nor warning SINN about sabotage would please the network or make up ground in a rapidly deteriorating relationship. And Will had made it clear that hooking up for national TV coverage was important not only for the tournament, but for his career—and for sudoku in general.

Liza also realized something Will either didn't have the words or the nerve to say out loud.

The only way to end this string of disasters was to find whoever was responsible and stop him, her, or it.

PART THREE:
Stung by Sudoku

What do you do when you really get stuck in a su-doku? I mean besides swearing and breaking your pencil?

There are two possible courses of action for calmer heads. One is to check whether the puzzle at hand is too complex for your skill set. Since Sudoku Nation still lacks a universal rating system, one puzzle-maker's "Medium" could be another sudoku-smith's "Hard." You may want to get hold of similarly rated puzzles from the same source and see how you fare.

Another approach is to walk away for a while. Make a clean copy of the puzzle clues, file the origi-nal somewhere, and put your attempted solution out of your mind. Give it a little time, and then try a fresh take at the copied puzzle. It may be that you made a mistake the first time around, but it hadn't shown up as a fatal flaw in your solution—yet.

If trying again brings success, you might want to compare your solutions to pinpoint your initial prob-lem.

If it doesn't work out, you can try, try yet again . . . or you can get the original and create some very decorative sudoku confetti.

—Excerpt from *Sudo-cues* by Liza K

11

When Liza told Will that she was thinking about solving his problem, he grabbed a seat and sank into it, staring at her. "But how can I—"

"We," she corrected.

"I know you've solved several murders," Will admitted. "But a whole string of events like this—"

"And kind of crazy ones, at that," Gemma put in.

"I think it would take a large organization to get to the bottom of them," Will went on. "An organization like the police. And if I—or we—went to them, it would let the cat out of the bag with SINN."

"Big organization or small, it comes down to the same things," Liza told them, "motive, opportunity, and means. My friends and I have been looking at motive—who might have a grudge against the people who died, or against you, or this resort . . . or maybe sudoku in general."

She paused with a frown. "That's a lot of ground to cover. Maybe we should focus on opportunity. Why is all this stuff happening here and now?"

Will nodded. "I see what you're saying. Well, the

tournament brings people from a fairly large geographic area together in one spot."

"And it brings them to this spot," Gemma added. "If someone had a grudge against the resort, this would be the perfect time to make trouble—I mean, with TV cameras on hand to spread it all over the country or the world."

"Two incidents did take place on camera, as it were," Will said. "Quirk's collapse and the grand unveiling that went awry. But poor Terhune getting poisoned—that happened at a private function."

"That would still be sure to get a lot of publicity after those first two episodes." Gemma turned to Liza. "Am I right?"

"And what about the incidents themselves?" Will objected. "Don't you feel it's a pretty big jump from petty sabotage—that what happened at the promo comes down to that, in spite of the scale—and killing people?"

"Not so big, if the person only expected to sicken the people who died," Liza argued. "I don't know how carefully you can measure out an allergen. Maybe the person just administered too large a dose. Whoever did it might have expected Quirk to choke or Scottie to puke, and just disrupt things."

"Which brings us to the question of means," Gemma said. "Attacking people through their allergies—that's kind of twisted. It also seems to suggest that whoever did it had a certain amount of knowledge about the people attending."

Liza nodded. "Ian Quirk was famous for trading on his allergies to get what he wanted in competitions. Scottie, though—I've known him for years, and I had no clue about any problem. Okay, he didn't want to go to any fish places, but I thought that was because he was a beer, burger, and fries kind of guy."

"That suggests that the perpetrator had to go to all the trouble of researching potential victims—and then got it wrong." Will's tidy mind evidently couldn't accept that.

"If I were you, Will, I'd worry more about myself," Gemma warned. "Do you have any allergies?"

Jolted, he stared at the actress. "Why—why, no."

"Because you definitely have enemies," Gemma went on. "That Quirk guy got pretty busy running you down, and his girlfriend Babs Whatsername is still doing a job on you. I've noticed her giving Fergus Fleming the old skunk-eye, too. If this went to a vote, she'd be my number one candidate."

Liza decided not to mention what she'd learned about Babs's last marriage. But she had to appreciate Gemma's view from the trenches of the dog-eat-dog entertainment business.

Will visibly shuddered at the thought of accusing Babs Basset of anything. "She'd have lawyers all over me," he muttered. But oddly when he looked at them again, he seemed much less agitated. "Whatever we do, we'll need irrefutable proof."

Liza figured it was the difference between failing to get any sort of grasp on a problem and having a plan, no matter how hazy.

Will took a deep breath, apparently free now to worry over other things. "At the moment, I have to deal with a more pressing problem. Roy Conklin has offered to give a talk on solving techniques this morning."

"Oh, right—he used preparing for that as an excuse not to attend last night," Liza said. "I thought he just wanted to avoid the crowd. Although, come to think of it, teaching a class doesn't exactly do that."

"He stipulated no more than forty participants." Will looked down at the table. "We've only had three people sign up."

"Well, perhaps I can help with that." Gemma rose from the table, leaving most of her breakfast uneaten. She just about dragged Will to the improvised food court in the lobby, with Liza trailing behind.

Joining the back of the line, Gemma turned on her actor's voice. "Coffee or tea for you, darling? And tell me more about that special class this morning. I'm definitely going."

Word spread quickly. Within fifteen minutes, the sign-up sheet was completely filled, with about a dozen more people on standby. Gemma insisted on adding Liza to the list. "Just in case there's any public relations to be handled," she said.

They had no problem finding the event room where Roy was speaking—it had a crowd in front. Liza spotted Roy peeking out the door with a mildly shell-shocked expression. Turning to hide a grin, she almost collided with Fergus Fleming, who strode down the hallway with a guy in a handyman's outfit.

"We've got a bunch of bees nesting under the roof overhang," he said. "I want you to figure out how we can smoke them out—do we need a ladder to come up from the ground, or can we get at them from the rooftop pool area?"

When she turned back, Liza found Roy gone—but the doors wide open and the participants filing in.

Actually, Roy's talk was pretty interesting. He used the puzzle from the ill-fated first round as a vehicle to discuss the various strategies. The attendees, especially those who had been stumped by the relative difficulty of Will's puzzle, probably learned something. For Liza it was stuff she'd all heard before and written about a lot. Still, it was interesting to hear someone else explore this familiar territory.

Roy's math background peeped out in some of the terminology he used. A puzzle became a matrix or an array. Candidates became variables, filling in answers became placements, things like naked pairs became conjugate pairs, and in one occasion, Roy referred to the whole solution as a subset.

Well, everybody's jargon was a little different. And bearing that in mind, Roy did a workmanlike job of running the puzzle and displaying the techniques most likely to lead to a solution.

Roy got a big hand, which made him blush. But he showed a teacher's skill in avoiding the people who wanted to make one more point and reaching Gemma and Liza. "Could we have a brief word?" he asked.

They ended up back on the patio, considerably emptier now that the breakfast rush was finished. Liza had managed to get coffee and some leftover pastries to make up for her drastically curtailed breakfast. Gemma had done the same.

Roy hid his cup of tea behind interlaced fingers, a look of chagrin on his boyish features. "I had a look at the sign-up sheet this morning," he said, "and when I saw you at my presentation—well, it didn't require a very long chain of logic to explain the suddenly packed house. I suppose I should thank you—no, that sounds ungracious. I *do* thank you for saving me some embarrassment."

Gemma gave him a smile. "I think I still hear a 'but' lurking around somewhere in the background." She shrugged. "It's just as I said when I first came here. It doesn't hurt to add a little celebrity to help a good cause—I've been involved in worse ones, I promise you."

He nodded. "I can understand that. Yet—"

" 'Yet' instead of 'but.' It comes out to the same thing, though," Gemma said with a bit more perception than Liza expected. "In a perfect world, wouldn't it be nice if the content of your brains—or your character—were enough to fill the house, instead of getting help from some movie star?"

"Well . . . yes. And no," Roy quickly added. "I didn't want to fill the house."

"You just wanted to talk about something that was important to you and have people hear it," Gemma said. "Unfortunately, this isn't a perfect world, and people want a little icing on everything—even broccoli, I think. Like it or not, Dr. Conklin—"

"Oh, please call me Roy," he said.

"Like it or not, Roy, attractiveness and celebrity have an effect on what you do, what I do, and what Liza does."

"Especially me," Liza said with a smile. "I'm in the business, after all."

"You're an attractive man," Gemma went on. "That didn't hurt you in putting over a fairly technical discussion on sudoku."

"I enjoy sudoku," Roy said. "For the general run of students, it's a nonthreatening way to do something with numbers. For the more mathematically minded, it's a springboard to more complicated topics. And for anybody, it's a way into logical thinking—strengthening mental muscles that don't get exercised, say, in a computer shoot-'em-up. I want to foster sudoku, promote it—"

He waved his hands in frustration. "But to do that, do I need to be an eccentric—a huckster, a diva, or a clown?"

"No," Gemma said. "But if you want to deal with the larger public, you do have to come to grips with celebrity, even if you keep it low-key."

Her perfect features took on a wry smile. "I'll talk about this in terms of my line of business, if you don't mind. It's what I've lived with . . . about as long as either of you have been alive.

"I started out as a kid model, and it was somewhere between playing and a job that helped bring in money for my family. Acting jobs seemed pretty much the same. When I got a bit older and had to start thinking of acting as a career, I began to see there were two kinds of people in front of the cameras in movies and TV. I called them actors and personalities. Actors portray different roles from project to project. Personalities generally play themselves— or what people believe them to be. That's not necessarily a bad thing—for a lot of people it's a dependable thing."

She frowned, trying to figure out her next words. "Then, there's the way you choose to interact with the public, whether you're approachable or unapproachable. For instance, do you court the gossip magazines and celebrity news shows? Being approachable means putting up with a lot of crap. Liza can tell you that."

"And how do you rate yourself?" Liza asked with some interest.

"Oh, I'm basically an unapproachable actor. I do different kinds of movies, there's a long time between visits when I do late-night TV, and I don't act as if my personal life is news." Gemma gave them a cynical smile. "Again,

Liza can explain how much publicity you can wring out of protecting your privacy."

Roy took a quick sip of his tea, pulling a face as if there weren't enough sugar in the cup. "I guess I can see what you're saying. But it seems awfully—"

"Cold-blooded?" Gemma finished for him. "It's a strategy, a logical chain of decisions where you try to stay as consistent as possible. So you end up becoming the guy who plays clever, handsome fellows and gets involved in one political cause after another. Or the ditzy blonde who's so adorable, she just about gets away with murder. I thought about being her for my career, but it gets a lot harder as you get older. You've got to find good, quirky roles, or you end up as a B-list character actor on TV."

She shrugged. "I really don't know how these strategies work outside of Hollywood. Maybe Liza could tell you. But I do know that if you're going to deal with more than your family, friends, and classes, you have to choose a strategy and stick with it."

Gemma smiled as if she were looking back at her own decision. "Just choose a line you can be comfortable with—you've heard the old saying about how once you can fake sincerity, you've got the system beat? If you can find a strategy that lets you be consistent, you can create a system. People will know what to expect, and you'll have a way to deal with them."

She leaned back, her face suddenly grim. "The only drawback is, the more famous you become, the less you can trust anyone around you."

12

Liza didn't know what to say to that. Luckily, she didn't have to. Mrs. H. appeared on the patio, looking around. Liza waved and took the opportunity to introduce her friend and neighbor to Gemma and Roy.

"You're up late," Liza said.

"That's because I was up later than usual last night," Mrs. Halvorsen replied. "I guess I'm not used to going out gallivanting in the evening."

"I'm sure you noticed the breakfast buffet in the lobby," Roy said. "Although I don't know if there's much left by now."

The older woman smiled. "I'm not one for loading my plate. A cup of tea and a piece of fruit will do. Then, I've got my book and my sun hat." The light straw brim gave a flutter as she spoke. "All I need is a pleasant place to sit while you do your puzzle, dear. Forgive me for not waiting for word with the others, but all that standing yesterday began to get to me."

"No problem, Mrs. H.," Liza said. "I brought you here so you could enjoy yourself. Take a rest."

"While the rest of us get ready to strain our brains,"

Gemma said, looking at her wristwatch. "I don't know if you have any last-minute things to take care of, but I do."

She rose, as did Roy, reminded of his own preparations. "I took a peek on the way here," he said. "We'll have two rooms for this round. And remember, the solving time is five minutes less."

"How could we forget?" Gemma asked as she walked back into the building. Liza trailed along while Mrs. Halvorsen chose the makings of a light breakfast, then Liza left as her neighbor went back out to the patio.

Heading back to her suite, Liza took care of the results of the two cups of coffee she'd drunk. She had no intention of trying competitive sudoku on a full bladder.

Then Liza washed up, ran a cool cloth across her face and behind her neck, toweled off, and went to the suite's sitting room. She could still enjoy a few minutes of quiet time, but she didn't quite trust herself to lie in bed.

Just my luck to drop off and snore through the competition, she thought, trying out the springs in the cushions on the large armchair. To quote Mrs. Halvorsen, it was not too "mooshy."

Liza settled herself and tried to blank her mind for a few minutes before getting up and preparing for battle. When she heard the door open, she turned with a little bit of irritation. *Hell of a time for the cleaning crew to show up,* she silently complained.

But she didn't see the housekeeper standing in the doorway. Instead, she saw Mrs. Halvorsen.

"Oh!" Mrs. H. said, flustered. "I didn't expect to find you here, dear. I thought you'd be downstairs already."

"I'm leaving in a minute," Liza replied. "And what about you? I thought you were going out to enjoy the California sunshine."

"To tell you the truth, that may be a bit too much of a good thing." Mrs. H. looked a little shaky as she put her book down. "Maybe I'm more used to gardening instead of just sitting in the sun. It seemed kind of glaring, and I felt a headache coming on."

Liza rose and patted her friend on the shoulder. "Well, then, take it easy. That's the whole reason you're here. There's nothing you have to do."

"Thanks, dear," Mrs. H. said gratefully as she headed for her bedroom.

"Unfortunately, the magic hour is approaching for me." Liza waved good-bye and headed downstairs.

She was surprised to see a new face getting powdered up in the makeup area. Humphrey Dunphy grimaced slightly as the makeup artist removed his bib. "This is something I didn't miss when I left San Francisco," he said. "Although it's a simpler job nowadays."

"How's that?" the makeup person asked.

"You didn't have to do any fancy shading to de-emphasize my jowls," Dunphy replied as he vacated the chair for Liza.

Once again, Liza found herself in the Hebrides Room. This time, however, Will was established up front with that abomination of a digital clock, and Dunphy had the end seat of the row just ahead of Liza.

Well, he's definitely arrived, she thought. *They not only made him up, but they put him in a space where the cameras will have easy access.*

She sat quietly as Will went through the revised rules for this round. They weren't all that different, except for the time limit. In the last round, the cutoff had been forty-five minutes. This time competitors had only forty minutes to complete the puzzle.

As Will finished, he gestured to a pair of volunteers, who quickly distributed the familiar sealed envelopes. Will stood looking at the watch on his left wrist, his right hand on the starting mechanism for the dreadful digital ticker. "Everyone ready? Prepare to start . . . now."

He hit the switch, and the numbers 40:00 flickered on the big screen. They quickly changed to 39:59, and Liza turned her attention to removing the puzzle sheet. She certainly couldn't describe it as sudoku for complete incompetents, but its difficulty pretty much matched the upper range of Sunday puzzles—the sort that people could spend a good part of their Sunday afternoon fooling around with.

Liza applied her techniques like a buzz saw, clearing away the forest to try to find the interesting trees. As she did, she veered between Roy Conklin's terms for the techniques and her own. Any conjugate pairs? Any pointing pairs?

She paused, debating whether to make another scan for the ever-elusive swordfish, and caught a glimpse of the timer. Ten minutes had passed. Liza didn't know whether she had expected more or less.

When she glanced over at Dunphy, she found him hunched over his puzzle. His attitude seemed a little stiff, and only when she sensed movement at the corner of her eye did Liza suddenly realize why. The camera crew was in the room, and they were filming him.

She quickly bent her eyes back to her paper, not wanting to be caught like a deer in the headlights should the lens suddenly turn her way. As she worked her way back into the puzzle, Liza couldn't help noticing the subdued noises coming around behind her. Great. Now she was the target.

Throughout the next twenty minutes or so, the camera crew spent most of its time peering over her shoulder or Dunphy's.

I guess we must be the front-runners in here. But Liza quickly repressed that thought. The secret to competitive sudoku was to avoid concentrating on the competition and put all your attention on the puzzle. That wasn't as easy to do with the almost subliminal distraction of the camera people, but Liza did her best.

Her pencil just about flashed along as she reached the point where the simplest techniques served to eliminate the pesky digits obscuring the remaining two-candidate spaces. And there it was—the solution.

Liza throttled back on a wild impulse to raise her hand and claim first place. That was the SINN crew's fault, making her feel as if she were in a race with Humphrey Dunphy.

Instead, she forced herself to check over the solution and then recheck it.

All right. *Now.*

She raised her hand, and a volunteer took the paper, bringing it up to Will. Liza left him to peruse it while she headed for the door.

Glancing back as she put her hand on the knob, she saw Will give her a quick nod. She also saw Dunphy's hand go up.

Liza ignored the hall monitor's shooing gestures and waited for Dunphy to emerge from the Hebrides Room. When he came through the door a moment later, he halted in surprise at finding Liza there.

He waited until the door shut behind him, and then whispered, "Well done, Ms. Kelly."

"Call me Liza," she told him. "And well done yourself."

"Just call me Doc," Dunphy replied. "That's the nickname the people in my gym gave me, and I decided to go with it. I was a lot more formal in San Francisco, for all the good it did me."

They walked along the hallway quietly, halting as another door opened. Babs Basset emerged and leaned heavily against the panel. From the sound she made, she might have been swallowing her own tongue.

"I hope that didn't make it onto the sound track," Dunphy said mildly as Babs almost ran down the corridor in full retreat.

"What's your relationship with her?" Liza asked.

"In a word, bad," Dunphy told her. "Babs Basset made me look like a big, fat sad sack. I suppose you heard I was run out of town. Actually, it was more in the way of being snickered out."

The muscular young man gave Liza a sidelong look. "So if she had been the one to grab her throat and hit the floor, I'd certainly be your prime suspect. Oh, yes," he said, raising a hand, "your reputation precedes you—in a nicer way than my gut used to precede me."

"From the looks of you, I'd expect you to break Babs over one knee," Liza told him.

Dunphy just shook his head. "I really do believe that living well is the best revenge. Although, to tell the truth, I just fell into it. The first job I could find that would get me out of dear old Frisco was in Phoenix, a town where I didn't know anybody. So, looking for something to do in the lonely evenings—and I guess kind of tired of my appearance—I joined a health club."

He patted his flat stomach. "And I ended up becoming quite the gym rat."

"But in the end you didn't give up on sudoku," Liza said.

The younger man shrugged. "As I got more into the social swing, I met a bunch of sudoku fans. Then a local reporter interviewed me—interestingly enough, they were doing a piece on his paper picking up your column. Print people began calling whenever they needed background, and even people from the local TV news operations. At first I sort of held back, even when they told me that I made a refreshing change from the average sudoku fan."

"Stereotypes at work," Liza said.

Dunphy nodded. "Then I got an invitation letter from Will Singleton, telling me about this tournament—and who would be here."

Almost reflexively, his right hand clasped into a fist so tight, the veins on the back of his hand stood out like bluish worms. "It would be nice to beat her, head to head, and to launch my new sudoku career."

Liza laughed. "You know, I've got a friend"—explaining Michael's status would be just a little too much on such short acquaintance—"who has started to talk about a Sudoku Mafia. I guess I should wish you good luck as the new don of Phoenix."

"Don Dunphy?" He made a face and shook his head again. "I think I'll stick with Doc."

They had almost reached the end of the corridor. Around the bend they could hear the muttered noise of the waiting crowd.

Dunphy stopped. "I'll wish you good luck, too, Liza. It would be nice to reel in the prize money, but I'd have to pull some amazing times in the last two puzzles to beat you."

His heavy shoulders rose and fell in a shrug. "For me, it will be enough to leave Babs baby in the dust." He grinned. "That would be living well indeed."

Liza let Dunphy go ahead of her into the room, causing a buzz of comment from the assembled sudoku fans. *The least I could do for Don Doc,* she thought.

As soon as Dunphy appeared in the doorway, Babs Basset all but fled the anteroom.

Her own appearance drew a smattering of applause, and Liza's little circle of friends quickly joined her.

"Well, you're definitely one of the big three," Kevin said.

"Bigger than you know." Liza explained the actual order of their exits.

"Hey, even better," Michael burst out exuberantly. "I put in a reservation for lunch at a nice place—I know you don't want anything too heavy—and now we have something to celebrate."

Kevin looked a little put out at being outmaneuvered by his rival, especially when Michael asked, "You think you can bend yourself into the backseat of a Honda, pal?"

Liza, however, ignored the Archie and Reggie–style back-and-forth. She concentrated on Mrs. Halvorsen, who still didn't seem at the top of her game.

Before Liza could ask anything, however, Will Singleton appeared. "The clock is still running down, but we already have five top scorers."

He proceeded to run down the list. "Roy Conklin."

He must have vanished again, Liza thought. *I guess he's still working through what Gemma told him about dealing with celebrity.*

"Liza Kelly." Kevin let out a cheer as her other friends immediately began patting her on the back.

"Dr. H. Dunphy." Liza nodded at that.

"Barbara Basset." Will paused for a moment, looking around in confusion. Obviously, he expected Babs to push forward and take her usual bow.

Reaching the end of his list, Will said, "Craig Lester." That was a name Liza didn't know, but he certainly had friends in the crowd. Excited applause broke out as a balding guy pumped a fist in the air, yelling, "Yippee!"

Liza, however, had no interest in whooping and hollering. She took Mrs. H. by the arm. "Are you okay?" she asked. "It looks as if your rest didn't do you much good."

Mrs. Halvorsen's lips quivered. "I was upset, and it didn't seem fair to tell you why right before you went off to the contest," she said. "But while I was out sitting in the sun—you remember that Mr. Roche? He came over, saying he wanted to talk with me."

Liza stared. "What did he want?"

"He had a lot of questions." Mrs. H. hesitated. "I don't like to say this about anyone, but I think that man is crazy!"

13

Mrs. Halvorsen's forthright comment got a stare from Michael. "Why would you say that?"

"Because I think he suspects Liza," Mrs. H. replied angrily. "That is definitely crazy in my book."

"This sounds like something we ought to discuss," Liza said, glancing around at all the fans. "Preferably outside the property."

The men worked together, clearing a path to get everyone through the crowd and out of the hotel. Then they packed into Michael's Honda. He drove a couple of miles to a pleasant but not overpowering little restaurant with a patio of its own. Liza enjoyed a salad featuring half an avocado stuffed with chicken salad. Kevin had a steak and red onion sandwich, Michael chose a pulled pork hoagie, and Mrs. H. selected cold poached salmon on a bed of tricolored salad.

The older woman picked at her meal until Liza couldn't stand it anymore. "Why do you think Roche suspects me?"

"From the moment he came up, he kept at me to change my story—as if I were telling some kind of lie," Mrs. Halvorsen complained. "That man wanted me to say that I'd been awake, that I'd seen you around our suite long before you said you got back."

She bristled just at the memory. "I don't know if he thought I was some poor old biddy who didn't have all her marbles, or if he decided he could scare me into saying whatever he wanted."

"And what exactly did he say?" Kevin asked.

"He told me, 'You can't avoid the truth. Sooner or later, it will come out that Liza Kelly wasn't away from Rancho Pacificano as long as she said she was. Either someone will have spotted that fancy car she rode off in driving in the wrong place at the wrong time, or we'll prove she got into the kitchen while she was supposedly off on that drive.'"

She shook her head. "Then he had the nerve to say, 'I'm trying to be nice about this, ma'am. The police won't be, once they find out.'"

Liza didn't realize how angry she was until she glanced down at her plate and saw how she'd mashed her avocado flat. Instant guacamole oozed out from under her fork as if she'd wounded her chicken salad and it was bleeding green blood.

"Well, *that* looks appetizing," Michael told her, taking in the mess on her plate.

"Somehow, I've lost my appetite," Liza replied grimly.

She didn't speak all the way back to Rancho Pacificano. Maybe she should have, because she was boiling by the time she made her way to Fergus Fleming's office.

He had a bigger room than Kevin used to run the Killamook Inn, and it was decorated very differently. Kevin had a lot of huntin', fishin', and hikin' memorabilia from his days as a guide before he started taking classes in hotel management and then putting them into practical application. He even had a bearskin rug on the floor, shot by his grandfather years ago.

Liza had to admit that she'd had some interesting fantasies about possible activities on that rug and had even teased Kevin about them.

Fergus Fleming's office, in contrast, had more of an

old-world look to it. Paintings hung on the walls, mainly landscapes featuring glens, lochs, and a lot of rocks. The skies, however, reminded Liza of that cleverly done ceiling in the Skye Room. The wall coverings (surprise!) were in plaid, with matching tartan patterns on the rugs and even on the upholstery of all the furniture not made of leather.

Fleming's desk wasn't all that large, an old-fashioned rolltop type that looked as if it had done a lot of traveling. Judging from the way the room was set up, the Scotsman did a lot of his business in a conversational area set up in front of what seemed to be a working fireplace. Two over-stuffed chairs flanked a low table.

That was the first thing Liza saw when she stormed in. She couldn't believe it when she glimpsed logs and kindling arranged on a pair of gleaming andirons.

What does he do, get the air-conditioning running at full blast before he lights that thing up? she wondered. *For at least half the year down here he could be starting brush fires.*

Fleming rose from behind his desk and came around to the conversation area. "Is there some sort of problem, Ms. Kelly?"

"Yes," Liza replied, "I've got a major problem with your house dick."

"Mr. Roche is an assistant manager," Fleming said. "Security does come under his purview, and I know he can sometimes be a bit zealous—"

Liza leaned right into the man's bearded face, a trick she had learned from Michelle. "When he starts badgering a woman old enough to be his mother so she'll give the kind of testimony he wants, I think that goes well beyond zealous, Mr. Fleming."

"You can't be serious, Ms. Kelly."

"As serious as a heart attack, Fleming—which is just about what Roche gave to my friend Mrs. Halvorsen. He caught her alone in your lovely gardens and began interrogating her. And when she didn't give the answers he wanted to hear, he tried intimidating her."

"You say your friend is a bit elderly. Perhaps she didn't understand what Oliver was asking. After all, he's a trained law enforcement professional."

"Who was forced to retire from the LAPD after he unsuccessfully attempted to railroad a suspect," Liza finished.

Fleming's lips tightened and his eyes got a bit flinty. "I was assured that was a mistake. He had excellent references—"

"From superior officers who were glad to pack him off before he became a complete media catastrophe for them," Liza shot in again.

"He also made a very good impression on several of the partners here at Rancho Pacificano," Fleming told her.

Liza could just imagine those partners—Orange County developers, conservative types who'd love giving a job to a guy that they'd consider a no-nonsense cop. She took a deep breath and tried to calm down a little. This also meant that Roche wasn't somebody Fleming had just hired. The managing partner had probably accepted Roche as part of a deal with the other people putting up money for the resort.

She met Fergus Fleming's eyes. He still regarded her with a constrained expression. "Roche told me about your reputation. He collected clipping files on all the specially invited participants in Mr. Singleton's tournament. After Mr. Quirk collapsed, he warned me that you might try to conduct your own investigation."

Liza lost it again. "And what the hell do you think he's doing, just observing everything from behind the potted palms? He was trying to scare up a witness—or just plain scare one—to contradict my statement about where I was yesterday afternoon."

"Your alibi," Fleming said.

"My statement to the police," Liza told him. "Where does Roche come off questioning your guests about that?"

" 'Guests' plural?"

"Almost as soon as Ian Quirk was rolled off to the

ambulance, Roche tried to pump Babs Basset for information."

A sort of convulsive shudder ran through the big Scotsman's frame. "Did he?"

"Not that he got very far with her," Liza had to admit. "But considering his previous research—and your personal history with the lady—do you think that was a good idea?"

Fleming sank into one of the armchairs, his hands gripping the overstuffed arms tightly enough to create dents in the upholstery. "I see that you know some of that personal history yourself."

He sighed. "Perhaps you've heard people refer to the hotel business as the hospitality industry?" he asked.

"My friend Kevin Shepard has mentioned it," Liza told him.

The resort manager nodded. "And I imagine you must know how proud Kevin is of that inn up in Oregon. Well, ever since I was a lad, I was fascinated by a business offering people hospitality. I set out to learn the trade, hoping I'd have the chance to show off my own brand of hospitality someday."

Liza gestured around the office. "It seems as if that time is now."

"So I'd hoped." His lips twisted under his whiskers. "I took some strange roads to get here—"

Through Babs Basset's bed, for instance, Liza couldn't help thinking.

"And I don't necessarily believe that Rancho Pacificano is the optimal location for what I hoped to do. Frankly, I think a more northerly location would be better. However, this is what was available, in terms of time frame and financial constraints, and here I am."

"Not many resorts of this caliber would allow TV cameras all over the place." There Liza spoke with a professional's knowledge.

Fleming nodded. "To be frank, we could use the publicity. By no means are we the only resort in Southern California. It's been hard to get ourselves established. I thought that hosting a nationally televised event would raise our profile—the SINN people talked about doing background shots all over the property to lead into the tournament events. Instead . . ."

Liza wouldn't have believed it possible, but his big hands squeezed the upholstery even more tightly. "It's been a complete disaster. SINN has actually cut down their coverage. And all anyone has seen of Rancho Pacificano is people apparently dropping dead at every opportunity."

That head of red hair drooped for a moment. Then Fleming brought it back up to face Liza. "Given the situation, I imagine I'd be glad for any investigation that brings an end to these incidents—professional or private."

Liza nodded in silence. Fleming wasn't going to rein in Roche. But he wasn't going to get in the way of her investigation, either.

She frowned as she headed up to her suite. Kevin, Michael, and Mrs. Halvorsen all stood gathered in the sitting room. Apparently Mrs. H. had been conducting a guided tour. She was just sliding open the glass panel offering admittance to their private terrace as Liza unlocked the suite door.

A gust of wind came through the opening, and Mrs. Halvorsen's sun hat flew off as if it had finally taken wing. "Oh!" the older woman said, her fingers an instant too late to catch the hat as it skimmed into the room and under the couch.

"No problem." Michael dropped to one knee as he retrieved the hat.

"So what luck?" Kevin asked, turning to Liza.

"This is a very nice view. Thanks for showing us," Michael interrupted, rising with the hat in his hands and a very odd expression on his face. "What kind of view does your room have, Kevin?"

Kevin stared at him, wondering if that wind had gone in one of Michael's ears and out the other. "It's not as nice as this one," he replied gruffly.

"Oh?" Michael pressed. "Is it on the other end of the building? Does it have a landward view?"

"It overlooks the back of the stables, all right?" Liza figured he'd have a hard time getting the words "manure pile" out from between his clenched teeth.

"Stables!" Michael echoed like a kid opening a Christmas present. "I didn't know they had horses here! Isn't that wonderful, Liza?"

"Oh?" Now it was Liza's turn to be taken aback.

Michael's voice took on a hearty, laughing tone. "You know how I love horses, dear. Every year we never missed the horse show in Santa Barbara."

As a wife, Liza had heard that tone before—usually when Michael was trying to convince her of something that wasn't true. And a yearly pilgrimage to Santa Barbara in search of horseflesh was definitely untrue. Michael was more likely to say he'd do that when horses fly.

A little belatedly, she took up the cue. "I wonder what kind of horses they'd have here. Do you think people board their own animals?"

Shrugging, Kevin went along. "I wouldn't be surprised. Did you know you can store your own wine here, to be delivered to your table when you eat?"

"Amazing." Michael stepped over to give Mrs. H. her hat, drew her inside, and slid the panel closed. "C'mon, what do you say we go take a look?"

He prattled on until they got on the elevator, where Liza turned to give him a look. But Michael astonished her by putting a finger to her lips, cutting off any questions.

After a little pressing, Kevin started telling a few stories about his equestrian experiences while they followed some back passageways and finally emerged from the building.

Liza's nose wrinkled as a slight gust of wind brought a distinct whiff of the stables.

"All right," she burst out, "what's the big idea of dragging us back here? These are good shoes, and I don't want to go stepping in any—"

"You remember the first time Buck Foreman came to Mrs. Halvorsen's house?" Michael interrupted, his voice mild.

"He was very impressive with all that machinery," Mrs. H. said. "And then he found that funny box."

Michael nodded. "The one that could pick up any conversations and transmit them about fifty feet away."

"Mr. Foreman put it on the floor and squashed it like a bug," Mrs. H. recalled.

Michael nodded again. "So it's a funny thing. When I got your hat, I noticed a box just like that stashed under your suite's couch."

14

Liza stared at Michael's face, trying to see if he was joking. He looked dead serious. "Are you sure about this?" she asked.

Michael shrugged. "As sure as I can be on a quick look. I didn't want to handle it, and I figured we'd be better off getting out of range before we started discussing it."

That made sense to Liza. If someone were spying on them, she could see several advantages in not advertising their knowledge to the eavesdropper.

Kevin burst out in anger. "Who the hell would be doing a thing like that?"

"I think we can narrow down the list a bit," Liza answered him. "We need someone with a background in investigation, a willingness to get their hands dirty, a driving need to get to the bottom of what's going on here, easy access to guests' rooms—oh, yes, and a desire to make me suspect number one."

"Oliver Roche," Mrs. Halvorsen said. "I told you that man was crazy."

"And maybe a very specialized kind of crazy, at that."

Michael frowned. "Has anybody ever heard of a condition called Munchausen's Syndrome?"

"Is that what happens when you smoke a little dope and then eat everything in the house?" Kevin asked a bit facetiously.

That earned him a look from Michael. "That's the munchies." He coughed, glancing at Mrs. H. "Or so I was told back in my younger days."

"I seem to remember a Baron von Münchhausen. He told a bunch of tall tales with himself as the hero."

Michael nodded. "Being a hero is at the root of Munchausen's Syndrome. People will go to dangerous lengths to make that dream come true. Volunteer firefighters will commit arson so they can heroically battle the blaze. Health care professionals will give patients an improper dose or the wrong meds so they can 'save' them." He raised his fingers to put little quote marks around the word "save."

"Poison them, you mean?" Mrs. Halvorsen burst out in amazement.

"You think Roche is doing something like that?" Kevin asked.

"That ties in with something Fergus Fleming told me when I talked with him," Liza said slowly. "Roche researched all of the invitees for the tournament. And he was the first responder when both Quirk and Scottie began showing symptoms."

"But if he wanted to be a hero . . ." Mrs. H. shook her head. "They both died."

Liza shrugged. "One of the things we keep wondering about is whether whoever is behind all this actually wanted the victims to die."

Kevin mutinously shook his head. "But when we said that, we were trying to tie in the sabotage to the tournament. That would have nothing to do with Roche wanting to be a hero."

"Maybe it's two different agendas, two different people," Michael said. "One tries to sabotage the tournament—"

"Or Will Singleton," Liza put in.

"The other poisons guests at the resort, hoping to save them—preferably in front of TV cameras."

Liza pursed her lips as if she'd just encountered a bad taste. "Or maybe he poisoned one guest, hoping to save him—and poisoned the other to cover himself."

Her friends all stared at her. "What?"

"When one person dies, you look into the motive, opportunity, and means of—well, let's call it a rational murder," Liza tried to explain. "When two people die, it starts to look like the work of a serial killer—some kind of nut. That leads to a whole different range of motives to distract the police. And in the meantime, Roche is beating his brains out, trying to hand the cops a perpetrator."

"Which in a way could be yet another facet of Munchausen's Syndrome," Michael said.

Liza looked at her watch. "The afternoon puzzle session is supposed to be at two-thirty. That leaves me a little time to rest and get ready. Why don't you guys take off until after the next round? Mrs. H. and I will take a look at this magic box."

"Which might just well turn out to be some sort of pest control device." From the glance Kevin shot at Michael, he seemed a little disappointed that the hypothetical device hadn't worked.

"Could be," Liza said. "If not, let's think of ways we might be able to use it."

When Liza and Mrs. Halvorsen returned to the suite, the older woman looked very self-conscious, engaging in a stream of nervous small talk while Liza peered under the couch at the box Michael had found. It did indeed look like one of the bugs Buck Foreman had detected and destroyed. Liza had to repress an urge to do the same.

Roche doesn't know that we stumbled upon one of his magic ears, she thought. *Wouldn't it be nice to work it into some sort of scheme for a little payback?*

After she got Mrs. H.'s promise to back up her alarm

clock, Liza lay down for a little bit, trying to get some rest and clear her mind before tackling the next leg of the competition. She didn't know what sort of surprises Will Singleton might have in store. All she knew was that the contestants would have less time to deal with them.

Liza got up, showered, and put on a new outfit. Out in the sitting room, Mrs. Halvorsen perched on an armchair with her book, whistling, tapping her fingers, and apparently turning pages at random.

"I've decided to stay in the room this afternoon, dear," she said the moment Liza came in. "As soon as you go, I'm putting the bolt on the door and reading out on the balcony. Or maybe I'll go into my room, lock the door there, and take a nap."

Liza grimaced at the way her friend was talking to the surveillance mike. At least she wasn't down on her knees in front of the couch, hollering into the damned thing.

"That all sounds very restful, Mrs. H." Liza smiled at her friend. "I guess I'll see you a bit later."

She made it to the improvised makeup station with plenty of time to spare. Was it her imagination, or was the makeup artist putting a bit more care into brushing on her powder and eyeliner? Liza hadn't really thought about it, but she'd managed to put herself into definite contention for the tournament prize.

Liza enjoyed that brief excitement, having it tempered soon enough as Babs Basset got into the next chair. "Well," she said with a breathy sort of sigh, "I had quite a nice game of tennis. The courts aren't bad, and the pro was a nice enough fellow. I do so believe in using the amenities wherever I go."

Even if they're managed by an ex-husband who gives you hives, Liza thought.

Babs just kept burbling on. "I get in some sun and a swim every day, too."

While I seem barely able to manage getting in my meals and some sleep. Liza grumpily made her way to the

Hebrides Room. But then, Babs wasn't trying to figure out who was making all the trouble. She just wanted to make hay from it.

Liza halted in the corridor, suddenly recalling Michael's comment about different agendas.

Just as quickly, she pushed the thought away. This wasn't the time for distraction, she told herself. This was time for sudoku.

Once again, Will sat ensconced in the front of the room with that dreadful timer. This time, Doc Dunphy wasn't in the ever-shrinking gathering. But when Liza glanced around, she saw Babs Basset taking a seat behind her.

Liza wondered if she'd have to worry about spitballs if it looked as if she were pulling ahead.

Will launched into his well-practiced spiel about the rules, emphasizing that for this round, contestants only had thirty-five minutes to complete their puzzles. Assistants distributed the sealed envelopes, Will counted down the seconds on his watch, he started the timer—and they were off.

Liza had done several pieces in her column about rating sudoku. Now she wished she could interview Will about his rating methods—specifically for this puzzle. It seemed to teeter on the brink of requiring the upper orders of technique, where the would-be solver had to create chains of logic that threatened to cross over the border into the forbidden zone of guesswork.

The question of whether she'd have to go beyond the swordfish managed to occupy enough of Liza's mind that she barely noticed the camera crews. They only crept back into her consciousness as she rushed into the home stretch, her pencil slashing across the puzzle to eliminate the final candidates with simpler techniques. Then, once again, she became aware of almost silent scuffling movements as the crew kept cutting back and forth between herself and Babs.

Somewhere, Charley Ormond sat in front of a bank of monitors, trying to create drama, suspense—at least for the viewers if not the contestants.

Liza had to bite her lip, fighting the urge to thrust her

face at the intrusive lens and snap, "It's sudoku, for god's sake, not a sword fight."

But she didn't need the phony tension or the exasperation jogging her mental elbow as she checked over her solution. Haste and anxiety could make a person overlook obvious mistakes.

She finished her inspection, went over the puzzle one more time, and then raised her hand.

Liza couldn't be sure, but she thought she heard Babs actually gnashing her teeth in the background.

Liza got halfway down the corridor toward the waiting area when she remembered her last thought in this hallway—Michael's comment about two agendas. Maybe the notion had planted itself in her subconscious while she wrestled with Will's sudoku. But now the idea leapt fully formed into the front of her mind as she greeted her friends.

"I've had an idea on how to turn those bugs to our own use," she told them in an undertone.

"And how exactly do you intend to do that?" Michael had enough experience with Liza's plans to be worried.

"I'll give the bugmeister a time and place to eavesdrop on a conversation between myself and Babs Basset," Liza replied. "In the course of that, I'll accuse her of sabotaging the tournament."

She nodded at Michael. "Remember what you said? Two agendas?"

Now Kevin began to look concerned. "And what if she's following one agenda and tries to kill you like Quirk and Terhune?"

"I'm not allergic enough to anything for that to happen." But on second thought, Liza had to admit that he might have a valid point. "I guess it wouldn't hurt to have two strong men in hiding somewhere nearby."

Grinning, Kevin slapped his lean but muscular chest. "Well, we've got one, but where will we find another?"

"I believe she meant me," Michael gritted out.

Liza left them to their wrangling as she cast an eye over

the sudoku fans. She quickly spotted Oliver Roche's shaved head. Even though he tried to place himself inconspicuously against a wall, his height put that shining beacon of a noggin above the crowd.

Okay. He wasn't all that far from the end of the hallway where the contestants entered. As long as Babs came for her usual shot of ego-boosting applause . . .

Liza headed for the threshold, and at the same time Babs Basset appeared, offering a professional smile and wave to her supporters. Moving to intercept the other woman before she could cross the anteroom, Liza caught her by the arm and steered her toward the nearby wall—and Oliver Roche.

"Babs," Liza said, trying to put a bit of menace into her tone, "I think the time has come for us to have a talk. A serious, private talk."

Babs looked a little surprised, and then she shrugged. "The rooftop pool is pretty empty at this time of day," she said. "That's why I like to go there for a swim and to work on my tan."

She glanced at Liza's hand gripping her arm. "They also have a hot water spa so you can relax some of those tense muscles. Shall we say half an hour?"

Babs swept on, and Liza headed back to her friends. Michael bent his head to speak softly. "Whatever you said, Roche just about had his ears flapping. He's hurried off already."

"I guess you'll have to give him a few minutes to bug the place, but then go check out the rooftop pool for somewhere you and Kevin can take cover." Liza sighed. "Meanwhile, I'll have to decide on buying a new swimsuit, or wearing the one I brought with me."

Rancho Pacificano boasted a small boutique selling resort outfits. She'd passed the sales display coming and going in the lobby and hadn't been impressed by the swimwear flaunted on a tanned and apparently anatomically correct mannequin. Checking out the sales stock didn't improve her first impression. All they had were a few brightly colored bits of material for placement in strategic areas. And apparently they were charging the same price per ounce as the local gold exchange.

Scowling, Liza went back upstairs. The suit she'd brought was meant for swimming, not parading around in.

The VIP pool occupied the top of the resort's main building, raised far above prying eyes. Through the decorative waist-high fence, Liza could see the waters of Newport Bay down and in the distance. She spotted no suspicious little boxes, and no one else up here except for Babs doing laps in the pool. Her golden hair was darkened and sleeked back by the water, making the woman's features seem sharper, almost predatory, as she looked up at Liza.

"I began to think you weren't coming," Babs said, swimming to a set of steps and emerging from the water.

Liza managed not to gawk like a hick at what the other woman wore—a collection of straps and scraps that would barely offer enough material to make a slingshot.

Babs might be petite and slim, but every bit was "cherce," as the line in the old movie went. And she obviously worked to enhance it.

Maybe she's on the lookout for hubby number four, and needs to keep the goods on display, Liza thought. In her sedate black one-piece, she might as well have the word "frump" beaded across her chest in brilliant zircons.

Picking up a huge, sumptuous-looking towel, Babs dried her hair, then threw the towel over her shoulders like a queen's stole. "Always refreshing. A nice swim, a sudoku puzzle, and a dependable pen—you never know when you'll need a little ink."

Babs bared her teeth in a predatory smile.

Who's baiting who? Liza wondered.

"Do try the spa," Babs said blandly. "I think it will do you a world of good."

Liza shot a suspicious glance at the bubbling water—what was it going to do? Dissolve her? Then she glanced around for any long-poled implements that might be used to push—and keep—her under.

Nothing.

She stepped into the spa, sighing. It was even warmer than the afternoon sun on her back. Almost against her will, her muscles loosened a little as the streams of bubbles tingled against her skin.

Liza looked up, but Babs didn't seem about to launch a sneak attack. She spread her towel on a nearby chaise and bent to retrieve a plastic bottle of suntan lotion, offering quite a view to a nonexistent audience as she did so.

"I have this made up for my exact skin tone," the woman explained, rubbing the oil onto all that exposed skin. "It—"

She broke off to wave away a bug of the flying variety—a bee, Liza realized.

Instead of buzzing off, the insect made straight for her palm.

Babs opened her mouth, but no sound emerged. She staggered back a little, cradling her stung hand in the other.

Liza heard more high-pitched humming—the agitated buzzing of more bees.

Above her near-naked body, Babs's face showed naked fear as she backed away from her winged assailants. But two and then two more came on like tiny dive-bombers, going for her arms, her stomach.

Liza heaved herself out of the spa as Babs reached the railing.

"Ge' 'em 'way!" Babs cried in a curiously choked voice. At the same moment, another bee arrowed in on a stinging run. Babs flinched back, hitting the fence at waist level, overbalancing.

Her arms went up, her legs went up . . .

And then she went over.

15

Liza's wet feet skittered along the concrete lip around the pool as she dashed for the low fence. She bent over, then straightened up quickly as she saw a tanned form sprawled on the rocks rising out of the bay.

"This wasn't what I planned," she muttered, closing her eyes.

Bad move. A second later, she heard a high, angry whine—and then a stabbing pain in her lower right eyelid.

Liza jumped back, yelling in agony. She cupped a hand over her wounded eye. *At least it didn't send me over the edge,* she thought.

The sound of running footsteps brought her around. Kevin and Michael dashed up, shouting, "What happened? Are you all right?"

"I'm stung," Liza told them, "and I think Babs is dead."

They halted at the fence, staring down. "Not good," Michael muttered.

Kevin gently peeled her cupped hand away. "Where is the sting?"

"Oh, man." Michael peered forward. "Right in the eyelid."

He reached forward until Kevin slapped his hand away. "Hey! The stinger's still in there. I was going to get it out—"

"And if you do it with your fingers, you'll end up squeezing more poison in," Kevin interrupted, digging in his back pocket for his wallet. He pulled out a credit card.

"What are you going to do, pay a doctor?" Michael asked.

"No, I'm going to do something useful." Kevin gently scraped the card beneath Liza's eye. "There. It's out now."

Liza felt glad for that, but she still hurt.

"I think we should get you out of here." Michael suddenly recoiled. "Yikes—more bees over here."

Liza's eye with the stung lid had gone teary and blurry. She shut it and peered around with her good one, spotting several bees. Even as she looked, one went into a dive-bombing run, swooping down to sting—a magazine?

She looked more carefully. This was no shiny magazine, it was a sudoku puzzle book soaked with Babs Basset's suntan oil. She'd dropped her bottle, leaving a puddle of oil that had lapped over to the book.

Squinting, Liza saw that it was a pretty simple puzzle. If Babs had started a solution, the oil had dissolved whatever she'd jotted in.

But why did the bees hate it? Another bee made a stinging attack on the blank space.

"Something weird is going on here," she told the guys. "Grab a towel and cover that up. And then I suppose we should call—"

Liza heard distant sirens coming toward them even as she finished her sentence with "the cops."

They made their way to the other side of the roof to see a small flotilla of police vehicles—unmarked cars as well as patrol units—racing down the drive to the main resort building. In moments, Pete Janacek; his tall, skinny colleague; and several uniformed officers came hustling onto the roof.

Behind them came Oliver Roche, waving a tape re-

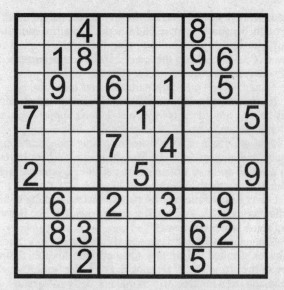

corder and yelling, "It's murder, Pete. There she is, and I've got proof that she did it."

His eyes had a feverish glint as he thrust his face forward, every muscle stretched tight. "The last thing the deceased said was 'Get away.' Then she screamed."

"Babs was trying to get the bees that were stinging her to stop," Liza replied, removing her hand from her eye. "I got stung, too, and there's something strange about that. I also saw bees attacking a puddle of Babs's suntan oil. We put a towel over it."

"I want pictures of that," Janacek told his beanpole partner. "Then I want that bottle to go to the lab."

The Sherlock Holmes look-alike had a supercilious expression as he got a crime-scene technician to remove the towel and take some pictures. Then he donned a pair of surgical gloves and picked up the bottle.

One of the winged insects buzzing around the puzzle

made the proverbial beeline for his hand and stung him
through the plastic glove. Old Sherlock lost his cool dis-
dain, yelping in pain and dropping the bottle. It splashed
some of its contents on the toe of his shoe, which immediately became another target for stings.

"You can't tell me that's natural," Liza told Janacek.

He sighed and told his assistant, "Try and bag that without getting any more on yourself. I don't suppose you're
allergic to bee stings?"

That got a scared look from the young man, and some
concerned glances for Liza. She shrugged. "Where I grew
up was half country. I managed to get stung by more things
than I could count."

Oliver Roche faltered a bit in his insistent shaking of his
little recorder. "Er—according to my research, Ms. Basset
had some insect bite issues."

"Something else for the medical examiner to look into,"
Janacek grunted, apparently finished with his initial sur-
vey of the crime scene. He took the recorder from Roche's
hand and used his free arm to make a "let's go" gesture to
Liza, Michael, and Kevin.

Liza immediately stepped over to a pile of those won-
derfully plush towels, chose one, and wrapped it around
herself like a mantle. "So, do I get a chance to change, or
will this be a come-as-you-are interrogation?"

Janacek went for the come-as-you-are variety, so Liza
handed him a couple of extra towels. When they established themselves in the Skye Room, she used the extras
to sit on so that her damp suit wouldn't soak into the upholstery on her chair. She'd thought that Janacek might
be amused, but he kept his face professionally expressionless.

Even so, it seemed to Liza that the painted sky on the
ceiling seemed considerably more threatening than the last
time she'd been in here.

The detective set Roche's tape recorder on the table between them, rewound, and then hit *Play*. The sound quality
wouldn't match the digital clarity of a film screening room,

but it was good enough. They could hear what had been said—including Babs Basset's last words.

"Not the clearest thing I ever heard," Janacek said heavily. "But I definitely made out 'get' and 'away.'"

"You couldn't really expect poor Babs to enunciate very carefully, given the circumstances," Liza responded, "but there's definitely an extra syllable between the two words. There were bees all around her, and she wanted me to 'get 'em away.'"

Janacek didn't say a word, using the growing silence to see if he could squeeze anything more out of his suspect.

"I don't know if Michael and Kevin were in earshot, but you might ask them what they heard."

"We're taking care of that," Sherlock Holmes snapped, cradling his stung hand. He shut up after Janacek shot him a look.

"You should put some ice on that," Liza told the younger man. She winced as her own sting gave a throb. "And I could use some ice for my eye."

Janacek dispatched his minion to the reopened kitchen, and Holmes returned with two bags of ice wrapped in damp napkins.

Liza sighed in relief as she applied the ice pack to the swelling below her eye.

Then she asked, "So what do you think, Detective? Did I get impatient that the bees weren't killing her off quickly enough, so I ran up and pushed Babs over—running into a cloud of angry bees to finish the job? Boy, I'd have to be pretty stupid to do that—especially when I knew the whole scene was on *Candid Microphone*."

Liza smiled as Janacek's expressionless face went downright stony. "Of course, you won't take my word about that. But you might ask Michael and Kevin. Michael was the one who came across the bug in the first place—well before this afternoon's round of competition."

She glanced over at Mr. Holmes, who looked torn between keeping his ice pack on his stung hand and putting it on his suddenly steaming head. "Better yet, you might go up to my suite and look for it. My friend Mrs. Halvorsen has just about barricaded herself up in there, but I'm sure if you showed her a badge, she'd be happy to point out where the bug is."

Her smile slipped a little. "Or maybe, if you asked nicely—or forcefully enough—Mr. Roche would actually admit to a little additional eavesdropping. By the way, Detective, what's the statutory situation here in Newport? Anything on the books about unlawful surveillance? I mean, it's not quite the same thing as setting up a camera in a changing room, but still, it comes across a bit . . . intrusive."

"Thank you, Ms. Kelly." Janacek's voice took on a grating tone she hadn't heard before. "You've given us several other things to check now." At his glance, the tall, young detective shot out of the room—*almost glad to escape,* Liza thought.

Janacek took in a lot of air and let it out, mainly through his nose. "So what were you doing up there on the roof, Ms. Kelly?"

Liza rearranged her towel around her shoulders. The ballroom's air-conditioning had been set for a much larger crowd than two, and she was feeling a bit chilly.

"I wanted to catch Babs alone," she said, "and ask her about the sabotage going on here at the tournament."

She explained how she had noticed Babs in close proximity to Will Singleton's portfolio right before the embarrassing unveiling stunt. "Will found definite traces of tampering. I thought I might use that to bait Babs into an admission, figuring it would be her word against mine— except her words would end up on Oliver Roche's tape."

Janacek took in some more air, but more sharply—in the form of a snort. "You are aware that this sabotage could also include a couple of murders, and a surveillance microphone might not be much help if you decided to bait a killer."

"Yes. Well." Liza fumbled a second for words. "That's why Kevin and Michael were hiding nearby."

The detective shot a glance at the compress she was holding to her eye. "Unh-humph," he said. "And that turned out just fine, didn't it?"

Liza felt her shoulders slump under her damp towel. "No it didn't," she admitted. "That bee attack and Babs falling—I was just hoping to get her off Will's back, and maybe scratch someone off the suspect list for the other stuff that's happened."

"She certainly got scratched off," Janacek muttered. More loudly, he said, "And I'm afraid her death—and what you just told me—make your friend Mr. Singleton a stronger suspect."

"That's crazy," Liza objected.

"Is it?" Janacek asked. "You yourself explained that Mr. Quirk and Ms. Basset were trying to undercut his position with the television people."

"If that's a serious motive, then half of Hollywood would be dead," Liza told him.

He gave her a mild nod. "In most circumstances, perhaps. But he might need the TV deal more than you're aware. We're looking into his financial situation now."

"And what about Scottie Terhune?" Liza demanded. "He's a friend of Will's."

"Maybe he was in the wrong place at the wrong time and saw something he shouldn't have. Something he might have inconveniently remembered at some point," Janacek suggested. "Or maybe he died because he and Singleton were friendly. Killing off a friend between two enemies—would that be a logical strategy for a mind devoted to creating puzzles to fool people?"

"That's not exactly—" Liza began.

"I guess you and Professor Conklin should be glad that you don't appear to have any allergies," the detective went on.

"Will is my friend," she snapped.

"And you'd trust him with your life?" Janacek smiled when she didn't answer. "Oh, it's just theory, Ms. Kelly. Take Mr. Fleming. Now he's a very pleasant gentleman,

running a local business, employees who look up to him—
and a wife that hated him. Now it might be a bit cold-
blooded to kill two strangers before doing in your wife."

"That wouldn't make sense at all," Liza objected. "It
would only serve to hurt his business."

"Or maybe Ms. Basset was behind the first two deaths,
ruining his business as you say, and Mr. Fleming used the
same method to do her in. Poetic justice, not to mention
tangling possible motives very neatly."

"You want to play theoretical games?" Liza said. "How
about this one?" She quickly outlined Michael's theory
pointing toward Oliver Roche.

That certainly shut the detective up. He sat very silently
for several minutes, just looking at Liza.

"I'm sorry," she said. "He must be a friend of yours,
judging from the way he called you so quickly."

Janacek nodded slowly. "But it is a theory, isn't it?
That's what happens when you have a definite lack of facts.
I'm afraid my plodding colleagues and I will have to do
some of that famously dull police work here. We've got too
many motives, and too many intersections at this location
to work out opportunity—"

The detective's cell phone rang. Excusing himself, Janacek opened it. "Yeah, Doc." He listened for a moment,
then asked, "And the bottle?" Another pause. "And what
did he say? Unh. Unh. Unh-huh." Thanking the doctor on
the other end, Janacek cut the connection.

Then he turned to Liza. "Some early information from
the ME. Doc says it's too close to call right now on cause
of death, the fall . . . or anaphylactic shock. Ms. Basset
was probably unconscious before she hit those rocks."

That was pretty horrible, but in a way Liza felt a little
better as she nodded.

"He also did some quick tests and found something that
didn't belong in that bottle of tanning goo," Janacek went
on. "He's not entirely sure yet, but it seems to be bee venom.
The doc called an entomologist friend who explained that
venom usually gets into the air after a bee stings some en-

emy and pulls her insides out. When other bees smell the venom, they get very aggressive and sting whatever they smell the venom on—even inanimate objects."

"Like Babs's book," Liza said.

"And it certainly pushes this investigation into looking at means." Janacek settled back in his seat.

"Things that set off people's allergies?" Liza gave him a doubtful look.

"Peanut candies aren't too hard to get—you might even take them along with you on a trip," the detective said. "And maybe you could pick up some shellfish juice—clam broth or the like—locally. Bee venom, though—where would you get that?"

Janacek's lips pressed together in a thoughtful scowl. "You flew in, Ms. Kelly, as did Dr. Dunphy—yes, we know about his history with Ms. Basset. Mr. Singleton also flew from New York, but he's been here several days making preparations . . . for the tournament," he finished after a perceptible pause.

"Professor Conklin took a winery tour before arriving in town here," the detective went on. "Fergus Fleming lives here on the property—as does Oliver Roche," he added heavily. "Your friend Mr. Shepard flew here, but your—what can I call him, your estranged husband?—he drove here from L.A."

"You can't be thinking—" Liza began.

"This isn't about thinking." Janacek cut her off, back in tough cop mode. "This is about proving. And if the neighbors say your husband set up a bee trap in the backyard, or he ordered a lot of steamed clams lately, we'd really start making a case."

"Or if you find out anything about any of the other people you mentioned," Liza pointed out.

Janacek nodded. "Of course."

After a quick knock on the door, Janacek's young partner came in, his Holmesian cool completely shattered. "There's a bunch of camera crews outside and, uh, this gentleman."

Liza immediately recognized the short, bald, pudgy figure of Alvin Hunzinger. The guy might look like Elmer Fudd, but his legal acumen had gotten him the nickname of "lawyer to the stars." Over the years he'd gotten a number of Markson Associates clients out of various police and judicial scrapes. Apparently Michelle had gotten wind of what had happened and dispatched him to Newport.

He immediately went into legal pit bull mode. "I trust you haven't waived any of your legal rights."

"And hello to you, Alvin." Turning, Liza brought the hand with the compress away from her eye.

Alvin stumbled back. "Good God!" he blurted out. "What have they done to you?"

16

At first, Liza thought Alvin was trying out some lawyerly humor. That hope pretty much went down in flames when she saw Janacek and Holmes both gawking at her in horror.

The décor of the Skye Room didn't run much to mirrors, and even those featured smoked glass with veins of gold in the background. That still allowed Liza to get a good look at herself. The bee sting below her eye had caused swelling, and the thin and delicate tissues of the lids and their surroundings hadn't liked that. Tiny blood vessels had ruptured, and even though it was less than an hour since the bee had attacked her, Liza wound up with the beginning of a glorious (or godawful, depending on your point of view) shiner.

Liza's personal opinion fell more on the godawful end of the spectrum, but she still had to hide a grin at the reflected expressions on the two police officers.

The tall, young cop's eyes zipped back and forth as if he were watching a tennis game on fast-forward—or trying to formulate a lie. He had been out of the room for a good deal of time and had no idea what Janacek might have gotten up to.

Janacek, on the other hand, looked even more stolid than usual, just a little more hunched in on himself, his lips downturned and pursed as if he were trying to decide if the latest bite he'd taken had some ingredient that had gone bad. He, too, realized that he'd been alone with Liza, and that this could easily turn into a very nasty case of she said/he said.

Liza turned to Alvin. "I was attacked—"

The lawyer stretched up to the tallest height his short, rotund form would allow.

"By a bee," Liza finished.

Alvin lost his height, his face scrunching up in confusion. "Is that some kind of slang I don't know about?" he asked.

Liza shook her head, winced, and reapplied the cold compress. "No, I'm talking about a real bee—the insect. An angry bee stung me up by the pool. Babs Basset got stung, too, before she fell off the rooftop."

"The deceased?" Alvin obviously knew that already. He was actually asking, "Is this our story, and are we sticking to it?"

"Those bees up there were acting way out of character," Liza went on, ignoring the cues Alvin was silently trying to give her. "Detective Janacek just got a call to that effect."

Janacek harrumphed, trying to hide the near heart attack Liza's initial words had almost given him. "Ah. Yes, Ms. Kelly. I think our business here is done for the time being. Perhaps sometime tomorrow you can stop by the station to give a formal statement—"

"And I'll be happy to accompany my client." Alvin maintained a steely tone, but from the look in his eyes, there went another tee time.

"I'd also request that you don't discuss any of our conversation with the media," Janacek went on.

"That might be interesting," Alvin said.

Liza glanced at him. "Just how many newspeople are out there?"

"There's a SINN camera crew, naturally," Alvin told her. "And crews from all four of the network news affiliates, plus a couple of local news stations. With three apparent murders in a row, people are bound to start taking notice."

"And I have to go out and face all that in a bathing suit, a towel, and this." Liza lowered her compress again, getting a wince out of all three men.

"Maybe some sunglasses?" Janacek fumbled in his jacket pockets. "I'm afraid I left mine in the car." He turned to his partner, who produced a very stylish pair of shades, with lenses so small as to be useless in actual sun, much less hiding the damage to Liza's eye. "From the Ben Franklin Collection, I see," she said, handing them back.

"You could use mine," Alvin began, producing a pair with lenses that, if anything, were oversized. But when Liza tried them on, she reeled slightly.

"They're prescription," Alvin explained, somewhat unnecessarily.

"But they do hide the eye." Liza peered into a mirror. Her view was blurred and a little crazy. She could make out that much, though.

She reached out to Alvin, missed, and tried again, this time linking her arm through his. "I think you'll have to lead me," she told him. "All we have to do is get to my suite."

"All right," he said a little nervously. "Don't say anything—let me do the talking."

"No problem on that," Liza told him. "I'll be too busy trying to navigate." She took a deep breath. "Shall we get going?"

Liza not only had to match her steps to Alvin's shorter stride, she had to bend down to rest her arm in his. Even as he opened the door, she was off balance.

They found the hallway outside the door filled with media people. Liza was used to the shouted questions, the blinding camera lights. However, she usually worked to protect clients, leading them past this circus. Instead, this time she was the focus of all the questions.

"Can you tell us why you were up on the roof with Babs Basset?"

"How exactly did she come to fall into the bay?"

"Why are you in a bathing suit?"

"Is it true that you threatened her while setting up a meeting?"

Liza simply concentrated on covering ground, leaving Alvin to tell the reporters, "No comment. Please let us pass."

One avid press person shoved a microphone into Alvin's face with some inane question, forcing the lawyer to break step and Liza to look down to see where she was going.

Very bad move. The sunglasses were bifocals, and Liza got a whole new distorted view of her feet. She stumbled, the towel went one way, and the glasses slipped off her nose.

The media people pounced like barracudas scenting fresh blood in the water.

"Liza, what happened to your eye?"

"Did Babs Basset do that to you?"

"Did the police?"

Alvin got them moving again, repeating his "No comment" mantra. Liza followed him half-blindly, squinting out between her swollen eyelids.

We're never going to make it down this corridor, much less to the elevator, she thought in dismay.

Suddenly, the door to one of the other event rooms swung open, and Fergus Fleming beckoned them in.

"Any port in a storm," Liza murmured into Alvin's ear, half-steering, half-stumbling toward the entrance.

They made it just before the media people could block them. Fleming firmly shut the door on the cameras and twisted the lock. He ran a hand across his eyes in delayed reaction to the camera lights. "Is that what they call a perp walk?" he asked, sounding exhausted.

"I think that would fall more under media frenzy," Liza told him. Then she introduced Alvin.

"I know of you by reputation, Mr. Hunzinger," Fleming said. His tone of voice definitely suggested that he sincerely hoped he wouldn't get to know Alvin in a professional sense.

"Liza's partner heard about her involvement in the situation here and thought she should have some legal advice," Alvin responded smoothly.

Liza glanced around for the makings of a new ice pack. She suspected Michelle Markson had been a good deal more peremptory about it, but she didn't see any reason to point that out.

"You look like hell, Liza," Gemma Vereker said, suddenly appearing and steering Liza toward a makeshift bar. She also smiled down at Alvin. "And how is the smoothest lawyer in Hollywood? He managed to fix things after a director of photography said some stupid things about me in front of a stunt man friend—a *large* stunt man friend."

"I just managed to find a couple of witnesses who said the director had been drinking and started the argument," Alvin said, but he flushed with pleasure as Gemma patted his arm.

Gemma shook her head as she surveyed the bar. "Only paper napkins here. They'll turn to mush as the ice melts, and you can't just put a cube directly onto your skin."

She turned as Kevin hustled up. "I should have expected that." He sounded annoyed with himself. "Is that the door to the kitchen?"

Fleming nodded, and Kevin headed off.

"You've got quite a congregation here," Liza told him.

"The police left me here after asking some questions. When the newspeople showed up, I figured it was just as wise to stay. Several other people showed up after talking with the detectives, so I decided to arrange a little hospitality."

"I came for the privacy and stayed for the free booze." Gemma picked up a bottle of single malt Scotch, refreshed Fleming's glass, then poured herself a healthy snifter.

"This probably won't be a good idea applied topically,"

she said to Liza. "But it might not be a bad idea taken internally."

Liza suspected that even half the dose Gemma had in her glass would be enough to lay her on the floor. She spotted a nearly full bottle of white wine in an ice bucket and poured a small glass for herself.

"Speaking of badmouthing, the cops heard that the Wicked Witch of Frisco had some choice things to say about me, so they asked some questions." She shrugged. "Luckily, I could honestly say that I really hadn't heard much." Her lips stretched in an evil grin. "All I could say is that I guessed she was growing a little desperate about getting her ass handed to her in the competition."

And since I'm one of the people doing that, the cops ended up looking at me more closely, Liza thought. *Thanks, Gemma.*

She took a sip of the wine.

"They asked me about how our marriage ended." Fleming lowered the contents of his glass pretty dramatically. "How did they think it ended?"

"I didn't know if I should mention something about a loss—"

Fleming's mood quickly shifted. "Whatever we had was dead long before whatever happened on the roof."

"I'm sure the police told you about that, if not Kevin and Michael." She'd spotted her former husband staring in horror at her eye.

"But you were there and actually saw it," Fleming said.

She gave him the bare facts with no interpretations—and no mention of the information Janacek had gotten.

Fleming shook his head. "She knew bees were dangerous for her. But instead of keeping still like a sensible person, she'd always try to wave them off."

I wonder if he mentioned that to Janacek—or any of the other cops, Liza thought.

Fleming retrieved the Scotch bottle, refilling his glass and topping off Gemma's. "Maybe it's selfish," he said heavily. "But all I can see coming out of this is damage for my business."

Either he's genuinely upset, or I'm seeing an Oscar-quality performance, Liza thought.

"My partner often says there's no such thing as good or bad publicity," she told Fleming, quoting one of Michelle's favorite aphorisms, "only publicity or none."

Gemma nodded. "She's got a point, Fergus."

Kevin came bustling over. "Here's an ice pack, and something else for that eye." He grinned. "I thought that Angus guy was going to come at me with a cleaver when I asked for it, but he finally came up with some meat tenderizer."

"Meat tenderizer?" Liza asked in disbelief. "Like, from the kitchen?"

"That's where I got it," Kevin replied with a grin. "You see, it has enzymes to break down protein—and that includes bee venom." As he spoke, he mixed in some water to the little pile of powder on a small saucer. Then he applied the paste carefully to the area under Liza's eye, his fingers surprisingly gentle as he worked. "When you go to bed, take an aspirin or some sort of analgesic—good for the pain. You can also take an antihistamine, too. That will help with the swelling." He glanced at the glass in Liza's hand.

"I just took a couple of sips," Liza said, putting the wine down. "As for the pills, I saw Mrs. H. unloading what looked like a traveling pharmacy in our room."

Gemma gave her a crooked grin. "That's our Liza, safe and sane—and I hope dependable. I'll certainly be depending on you tomorrow morning."

"Before I can put myself to bed, I've got to get up to my room." Liza beckoned Michael over. "Can you get up to Mrs. Halvorsen and have her send me down some clothes? I'm going to look a little conspicuous trying to sneak around the hallways dressed as I am."

"Especially with all those newspeople out there." Michael frowned for a second, then said, "Kevin said he came back from the kitchen, but he didn't come through that door."

"There's a back hallway connecting each of the event rooms with the kitchen," Fergus Fleming explained.

"Then that's my way out—yours, too, Liza, when I get back."

Soon enough, Liza had changed into some nice, nondescript clothes and had a pair of sunglasses that didn't make the world look like a funhouse. As she said good night to everyone, Gemma said a little blurrily, "G'luck. An' remember to get me in the morning," apparently forgetting she'd already asked.

Liza emerged from the kitchen to an empty hallway and quietly headed off to the elevator bank. She made it upstairs with no excitement, except for the fuss Mrs. H. made when Liza finally got to their suite.

It seemed that Michael had reported at least part of the story to Mrs. H., because she had a fresh supply of ice for compresses. She'd also sorted through her pill bottles for the appropriate nostrums. Liza let her neighbor play mother hen all the way to her bedroom. To tell the truth, she felt exhausted, but she forced herself to take a shower to get the dried chlorine off her. Mrs. H. had already turned down the covers, and Liza just about fell in. She didn't even remember the light going off.

By morning, the pain was down, but the bruise remained like a big, dark thundercloud under her eye. Liza winced at her reflection. Mrs. Halvorsen, though, sounded encouraging when she saw Liza in her sunglasses. "You can't tell a thing, dear."

The older woman insisted on accompanying Liza, ready to run interference with any rogue camera crews they might encounter. Liza, however, put her faith in the news cycle. There's always another story for a crew to cover.

They'd reached the lobby before she remembered her promise to Gemma Vereker. "I've got to go back up," Liza told Mrs. H. "Could you get yourself a cup of tea and a nice table out on the patio, and we'll join you."

The elevator doors were just closing when Michael scooted inside. "I wanted to check in and see how you were doing." He peered in from the side of Liza's shades. "Looks like Kevin's miracle cure didn't work much in the way of miracles."

"But I'm feeling much better—thanks for asking," she shot back in some annoyance.

"So what are you doing?"

"A part of my old job that you always especially hated."

"Ah," Michael said. "Lackey to the rich and famous. Did Gemma miss her wake-up call?"

"She asked me to stop in." Liza realized that part of her grumpy mood came from the fact that this was also one of her least favorite parts of her old publicity job.

They got off on the third floor and walked down several hallways to Gemma's room. Liza knocked but didn't get an answer.

"Yesterday morning, she was up, if not exactly bushy-tailed," Liza said.

Michael shrugged. "But she hadn't spent the previous night making a serious dent in Fergus Fleming's private whiskey stock. I thought for a while she was going to drink him under the table."

Liza frowned and rapped more insistently on the door. Then she dug out her cell phone and called the front desk.

"Well, yes, ma'am, we did make a wake-up call for Ms. Vereker," the young man at the desk replied, "but I'm afraid she didn't pick up."

Liza's frown only got deeper. "They couldn't get through to her, either," she told Michael. Then, speaking back into the phone, she asked if they could connect her to Fergus Fleming.

The resort manager sounded a bit morning-after himself, but as Liza spoke with him, he obviously made an effort to rally. "Stay at her door," he told Liza. "I'll be there in a moment."

When he arrived, his big, florid face looked a bit more pouchy than usual. But his eyes were clear and serious as he produced a red passcard. "The master key," he said, slipping it into Gemma's lock.

The tiny indicator lights over the handle went green, and he gently twisted it to open the door. A breath of somewhat stuffy air wafted out at them, and the sitting room was dim, the lights off, and the windows still shrouded with heavy drapes.

"Ms. Vereker," Fleming called gently. "Gemma?"

They stepped inside, Liza glancing around. The place was a little more disheveled than the previous morning. Gemma certainly made full use of the resort's maid service. The actress's purse lay casually discarded on the same table, its contents spilling out. Liza again noticed that sudoku puzzle with its near-catalog of rookie mistakes.

Fleming moved farther into the room, toward the bedroom, whose door stood slightly ajar.

"Pardon us for intruding," the manager announced a bit more loudly, "but you're going to miss the next round of the tournament if you stay in bed."

He paused in the doorway and called again, "Gemma?" Then he shook his head. "Sleeping it off, I guess."

Michael stood beside him to peer in. "Dead to the world."

Liza didn't so much look as listen. "Bad choice of words," she told Michael. "I don't think she's breathing."

17

Fergus Fleming recoiled from the door, muttering, "Oh, Lord, not again."

Liza grabbed Michael by the arm. "Come on. We're going in."

Michael resisted for a moment, then shrugged and let Liza lead him. "Don't go touching things," he warned.

She rushed ahead. Maybe she was wrong. Maybe something had just happened and they could help.

Liza dropped to one knee beside the bed, reaching out to touch Gemma's shoulder through the bedsheet. She shuddered a little, yanking her hand back when she didn't feel warmth. The cool girl she'd once watched on TV had grown too, too cool.

"I don't see anything," Michael began, only to have a violent sneeze interrupt his words.

He took a step closer to the bed and sneezed again.

"The other people who died were killed by their allergies." Liza frowned, looking up at Michael. "And you have allergies."

"To dogs, yes." Michael unsuccessfully stifled another

sneeze. "You know how I've been since you adopted that mutt."

"Rusty is a good dog," Liza said.

"Yeah, good for antihistamine sales." Michael sneezed yet again, then sighed. "When I was younger, some plants used to set me off."

"Well, I don't hear a dog, and there are no plants here." Liza looked back at the door and Fergus Fleming. "Gemma thanked Fergus for arranging that."

"There's got to be something." Michael dropped to his knee beside her, nearly falling over from his next sneeze.

"And I think you're getting closer." Liza looked around but, aside from the mess, didn't see anything out of the ordinary. She twitched up the bed skirt, and Michael came close to blowing out her eardrum with a "Ker-CHOOOO!" of near-volcanic proportions.

He only got worse as she held up the length of fabric and peered under the bed.

If the room was dim, this was downright dark. It took her a moment to make out the shape down there . . .

"Is that a tumbleweed?" Liza asked in disbelief.

Michael looked and staggered back, sneezing. "Either that, or the biggest dust bunny I've ever seen in my life."

Fergus Fleming had stationed himself at the outside door of the suite, working his cell phone for all it was worth.

A familiar face passed by in the hallway, stopped, and peered inside. "Is everything okay?" Doc Dunphy asked. The moment he poked his nose inside the room, his chiseled face changed, getting pinched. He vented a sneeze as loud as any Michael had produced. And when he asked, "What's going on?" his voice came out as a wheeze.

Fleming all but pushed him down the hallway. "Mr. Roche should be coming out of the elevator." The resort manager spoke very loud and very fast. "Have him check you out. If the symptoms persist, he'll know what to do."

He slammed the door shut and leaned against it as if he were trying to hold back the world from getting in. Seeing Michael and Liza standing in the other doorway staring at him, he straightened up and gave them a self-conscious smile. "We got some of those EpiPens—a single dose of epinephrine to counteract the anaphylactic shock."

Then he slumped against the door. "Not that it helped with Babs . . . or here, for that matter."

"What was that quote?" Michael asked. "The best-laid plans—"

"Of mice and men aft gang agley," Fleming finished for him.

"Robert Burns." Liza sighed. "Well, I'm afraid one of my hopes has gang agley."

Michael stared. "What's that?"

"Doc Dunphy was one of my prime candidates for this string of killings," Liza admitted.

"Why in God's name would he kill four people?" Fleming burst out.

"He had a grudge. Babs Basset turned his life upside down. And she did it by getting people to laugh at him," Liza responded.

"That would explain going after Babs," Fleming objected. "But the rest?"

"Cover," Liza said. "If just Babs died, the cops would be all over him. But the others, dying before and after, confuse the motive."

"But to kill . . ." Michael broke off, shaking his head.

"He didn't know them, and from the way I saw him act with Babs, he had a vengeful streak." Liza stomped into the sitting room. "He would have been a perfect suspect. But you saw him out there. Whatever was making you sneeze hit him even harder—his throat was closing down."

Fleming shuddered. "We don't need any more, thank you."

"So how could he have brought the tumbleweed in here?" Liza asked. "Unless he did it in a hazmat suit—"

Michael laughed grimly. "That's a great image," he said. "I think I can use that in the script for *The Surreal Killer.*"

"It would make him a little bit conspicuous here in the

resort." Liza's voice faltered as the full weight of Gemma's death finally hit her. Quirk and Babs she hardly knew, and while she was fond of Scottie, she didn't see all that much of him. But she'd idolized Gemma as a kid and then did a lot of work with her. It was just hard to believe . . .

Fleming's voice broke in on the sudden, sad silence. "So it's not Dunphy." Fleming spoke with a curious mixture of disappointment and relief.

"Well, I'm sure the cops will want to try him out with whatever is coming off that tumbleweed." Liza glanced back at the bedroom. "So you may need that EpiPen after all." She sighed again. "But otherwise—"

She looked down and frowned, realizing she stood beside the table with Gemma's purse on it.

"What's the matter?" Michael asked.

"Something else that doesn't fit." She looked up. "Have you got paper and pen with you?"

"What would you expect from a professional writer?" Michael produced a small notebook from his back pocket and a mechanical pencil. "Will these do?"

Liza took them and made a quick and dirty copy of the botched sudoku, marking blank spaces with an X, circling the clues, and leaving the mistaken entries as plain numbers.

When she saw Michael's quizzical expression, she shrugged, saying, "You told me not to touch anything. I guess that goes double for actually taking things."

"But what is it for?" Michael looked down his nose at the puzzle. "It's all screwed up."

"And it leads to some questions that need asking," Liza replied. "Questions that Detective Janacek will be too busy to deal with."

As if her comment were magic, an authoritative knock sounded on the door. "Police! Open up!" a voice called.

Fleming opened the door, and a pair of young police officers came in to secure the area. Detective Janacek just stood in the doorway. He didn't look authoritative—more like someone struggling for a long-suffering expression. "Ms. Kelly," he said. "What a surprise to see you here."

His voice, usually quiet, came across as almost toneless. Liza could understand why. This case was rapidly turning into the perfect storm for a police career—an upscale locale, possible serial murders, and now a dead Hollywood celebrity.

"We had to race the news vans to get here." That toneless voice wasn't so much Janacek giving up—it was Janacek trying to keep his temper.

"Now," the detective said, "would you mind explaining what you're doing here?"

Liza told him how she'd been recruited to back up Gemma's wake-up call, how she, Michael, and Fleming had wound up in the suite—and what they'd found.

Janacek's expression was back to nonplussed by the time Liza related her final discovery. "A tumbleweed?" he repeated in disbelief.

"Michael has some allergies, and it started him off sneezing," Liza said. "And Doc Dunphy just looked in the outer door and started to wheeze."

Shaking his head, Janacek dug out his cell phone and called the coroner, who referred him to an allergist. After a few questions and listening to the answers, he clicked the phone shut with a bemused expression. "People are indeed allergic to tumbleweeds, and sometimes the symptoms can become serious. In an enclosed space—say, a bedroom for example . . ."

"And in Gemma's case, it would be an even bet whether she fell asleep at night or just passed out," Michael added.

"So she wouldn't be aware of any distress." Liza bit her lip. "This just gets uglier and uglier."

While the crime-scene people got busy in the bedroom, Janacek glanced around the rest of the suite.

"What's your take on Ms. Vereker?" he asked Liza. "Was she usually this . . . messy?"

"I really can't say," Liza replied. "The place was neater

when I came to get her yesterday morning. But she was up and may have tidied a little."

Janacek frowned. "Or someone may have tried to toss the place. I'll have to get the fingerprint people in here."

Liza said nothing, but she thought, *That doesn't fit in with what happened with the other people who got killed—does it?*

"We may have more questions for you, depending on what else we find here," the police detective said. "Better leave now before the cameras make it up here."

Outside in the hallway, Michael started for Liza's suite. "We'd better tell Mrs. H. and get Kevin on board—" He paused as his companion suddenly stopped at the elevator.

"Could you take care of that?" Liza asked. "I want to give Will a heads-up." She pushed her thumb against the button with a little more force than necessary. "And maybe get some answers."

Luck was with her—she caught Will having a breakfast meeting with some of the tournament volunteers. Liza ruthlessly chased away the acolytes and gave him the news straight.

"Gemma Vereker is dead?" Will echoed, his face going as gray as his beard.

"And it wasn't an accident," Liza went on in a low voice. "Somebody found out that she had an allergy—"

"This is just too much." Will stared down at the untouched food on his plate. "Maybe it's time to cancel the whole tournament."

Liza knew that decision would have serious consequences not just for Will but for his media partners at SINN. "It's a tragedy, but maybe you could consider a postponement," she said.

"This is Sunday, and we only have the resort for the weekend. How far can I push things back?" Will burst out. But a thoughtful look overtook the pained expression on his face. "Maybe if we brought things down to a final round—sudden death—"

He broke off with a grimace.

"Not the best turn of phrase," Liza diplomatically admitted. "How about calling it 'Winner Takes All'? That might encourage some of the participants who are trailing in the rankings to bring their best games."

Will shook his head in admiration. "You always come up with just the right thing," he said. "How can I thank you?"

"You could answer a question for me." She reached into her pocket and brought out the sudoku she'd copied.

Will frowned in puzzlement. "Not exactly up to your usual standard," he quipped.

"The original is in Gemma Vereker's sitting room. It's a puzzle from one of those in-flight magazines. For all I know, you came up with it. The interesting thing, though, is that all those mistakes are in Gemma's handwriting. So here's my question. If that's the level of Gemma's sudoku skills, how the hell did she manage to keep placing in this tournament? Or was she getting a little help because of her publicity value?"

Will's face tightened. "I should think you know me better than that," he told Liza. "Everyone competes on a level playing field. I don't play favorites for publicity's sake. We've kept every completed puzzle that got turned in, time-stamped. You obviously know Gemma's handwriting, so you'll be able to see that she worked each puzzle out—and you'll see the pencil marks she made while she was doing it."

In other words, Will didn't just give her a puzzle to copy over. Gemma might do that. But somehow, Liza couldn't see Gemma making all the fiddly marks and erasures involved in duplicating a real solution.

"If she could do so well, how do you explain such poor performance on this puzzle?" Liza asked.

Will shook his head. "She's—she was—a very strange person, Liza. Maybe she was flying without the benefit of a plane when she did that puzzle. Or maybe she needed a couple of drinks to get into her sudoku groove, and that's how she did when she was cold sober."

He raised a hand. "I'm sorry, I shouldn't be so flippant about someone who's just died. So all I can say is that I have no explanation. As far as I could see, she was good, Liza. Maybe not up to your level, or Dunphy's, or Quirk's, or Terhune's, but she was way past novice level. Gemma Vereker didn't need any help to stay in contention."

Even with his facial fur, Will looked totally sincere. Liza apologized for her doubts and let him get to work publicizing the postponement and the new final round. She headed down the hallway, taking the opposite direction from her usual post-competition route. In between quick bites of breakfast, she'd given Michael a message for Kevin and Mrs. H., telling them to wait for her in the suite.

As she took a couple of turns, Liza thought, *This must be how Roy Conklin avoids the crowds.*

Right now, she was more concerned with avoiding wandering newspeople with camera crews and moronic questions.

The alternate route brought her to a corner of the resort building's main lobby, not too far from the elevators. As Liza checked out the space for media people, she spotted a familiar figure heading for the reception desk. There was no mistaking that roadkill toupee on Artie Kahn's head.

He approached the young woman behind the desk and said, "I called a little earlier—I'm Gemma Vereker's manager."

The young staffer gave him a serious-faced nod. "I'm afraid I'll have to refer you to Mr. Fleming, our manager."

"So the report I heard on the radio is true." Kahn's voice was heavy. "Gemma has no close family anymore. Has anyone made arrangements?"

The young woman repeated, "You'll really have to speak with Mr. Fleming." In the face of Kahn's obvious upset, she unbent a little as she picked up her phone. "The police removed the . . . remains. I expect you'll have to contact the coroner's office."

Kahn nodded. "I don't suppose—Ms. Vereker was coming to discuss some business affairs with me and had some important papers."

The girl behind the desk shook her head. "I'm afraid the police have sealed her room—"

"Of course," Artie said quickly. "I was wondering, though, if she might have left them in your safe."

"The resort maintains safe-deposit facilities for all guests." The words came out of the receptionist like a well-rehearsed speech. Then she hesitated. "I suppose I could look up—"

A few quick keystrokes, a glance at her computer monitor, and she shook her head. "I'm sorry, sir," she said. "Ms. Vereker didn't place anything in our depository."

Kahn nodded. "I don't suppose there's a safe in her suite?"

"No, sir, we encourage all guests to use our secure area."

Another phrase from her training, Liza thought as the young woman went back to the reception phone. Moments later, Fergus Fleming appeared.

Liza decided she didn't need any more lessons in hotel protocol. She stepped over to the elevators and pressed the *Up* button.

Almost immediately, the doors opened to reveal Oliver Roche about to step out. Both he and Liza involuntarily stepped back. But the hotel detective quickly recovered, looming over Liza, eyes glaring, his face so tight the muscles beneath the skin were quivering.

"Think you made a fool of me, huh?" His words came out between clenched teeth. "Maybe Fleming and even Janacek are swallowing your line of guff. But I've got your number."

He pushed past her to join the group by reception.

PART FOUR:
Sudoku on the Rocks

I always think the endgame is where most people encounter the real heartbreak of sudoku. You've rocketed past the X-wings, you've nailed the wily swordfish in its lair, and now it's just a case of using the really simple techniques to clean out the few remaining clues down to the one true number in each space.

Smooth sailing—until you hit a rock. You're down to a single 3 in the space at one end of a row, and there's a space with the same single number at the other end. That means that somewhere in one of the other seventy-nine spaces, maybe twenty moves ago, you made a mistake.

This is sudoku, after all. You can't have more than one solution . . .

—Excerpt from *Sudo-cues* by Liza K

18

Liza jumped into the elevator and stabbed at the button with her finger. She didn't let out her breath until the doors closed. Then she flopped back against the far wall, glad the car was empty. She rode up to her floor and walked directly to her suite.

Michael had the door open even as she slipped in her key card.

"Sorry," he said at Liza's startled expression. "We've been sort of sitting on the edge of our seats here."

When she got inside and saw the others all gathered around the telephone, Liza had a sudden hunch. "Is Michelle on the speaker?" she asked in a low voice.

Not low enough. "Liza? You took your time." Michelle's voice sounded all too familiar, even if it seemed to be coming from the bottom of a barrel.

"About this business with Gemma." Michelle had more important fish to fry rather than waste time with small talk. "I appreciate how quickly you let me know."

Liza had called her partner as soon as she and Michael left Gemma's room. Just the thought of Michelle's reaction to being out of the loop on such important information left Liza shuddering.

"I thought we might discuss the latest developments in the case, and I asked Buck to join in." Michelle's tone just about said out loud, "Time to bring out the big guns."

"Hey, Liza." Buck's deep voice came over the connection. "Can't have been nice finding another dead body."

"What's strange is how Gemma got that way." Liza explained what they'd found under the bed.

"Kind of early in the year for tumbleweed," Buck said.

"How would you know that?" Michael couldn't help his question.

"Got a friend who has the same allergy—not as bad as Ms. Vereker's, though," Buck replied. "The trouble period comes in late summer. So we might have an angle to work—where the hell did this thing come from?"

"Here's another angle," Liza suggested. "We never really publicized Gemma's allergic attack on the set of that Western."

"That's true. Gemma had reached an age where she felt a little—vulnerable—admitting to any physical problems," Michelle said. "Although she didn't mind playing up the back spasms from her rather athletic love scene in that noir mystery."

"Difference between a physical defect and a sports injury." Buck's tone was remarkably dry as he spoke.

"The thing is, it's not well known," Liza argued. "I don't think our killer went online to Celebrity Allergies Dot Com—"

"Wouldn't bet on that not existing," Buck warned. "Lot of strange websites out there."

"Huh." Kevin spoke up. "So the killer knows about sudoku pros and movie stars. Not much overlap there."

"Certainly not on the same website," Michael agreed with a frown. "And the killer would have to learn about Gemma's allergy pretty damn quick. Unlike the others, she came in as a bit of a surprise."

"Thanks for those very interesting conjectures," Michelle

said in her "let's move on" voice. "What can you tell me about suspects?"

"My favorite seems to have died already," Liza admitted. "Babs Basset had a vested interest in causing trouble." She sighed. "With Babs dead, the two front-runners would be Will Singleton and Dunphy. They both have fairly strong motives for killing her. But I have a hard time believing that either of them would go in for wholesale murder just to get one person."

"And Dunphy sort of disqualified himself with that allergy attack at Gemma's door," Michael put in.

"Sounds bad for your friend Will," Michelle said.

"Will Singleton has put his heart and soul into this tournament for two years. He hopes to turn it into a national event. It will be part of his legacy. I can't see him trashing it—"

"There's no such thing as bad publicity," Michelle said.

"It wouldn't exactly be good publicity for him to end up in prison for murder," Liza retorted.

"Well, do you have any other suspects?"

"There's one," Michael offered. He repeated his idea about Roche trying to be a hero, failing, and trying to cover it up.

"That's very much a screenwriter's theory," Michelle said.

"Do you have anything to back it up?" Buck asked. "Any connection to the last two deaths?"

"Well, he was the big cheerleader to get Liza arrested when Babs Basset died," Michael said. "She turned that around, but—"

"He threatened me," Liza said.

That got the room pretty quiet as everyone stared at her. For all she knew, Michelle and Buck were staring at their phone, too.

"When was this?" Kevin wanted to know.

"Just now as I was getting in the elevator. I thought his head was about to explode when he stuck his face in mine and said he had—"

Her voice changed as she finished, "My 'number.'"

Liza dug in her pocket and brought out the slightly crumpled copy of Gemma Vereker's messed-up puzzle.

Michael bent forward to peer. "Is that the puzzle you copied from Gemma's room?"

"What puzzle is this?" Michelle's tone sharpened.

Liza explained about spotting the puzzle torn from the magazine with its catalog of rookie mistakes, and Will's assurance that Gemma's skills were much better than that.

"And you believe him?" Michelle asked.

"Boy, are you giving him a bum rap," Liza said. "He's a murderer, a liar . . ." She broke off. "Yes, I do."

Kevin frowned. "So why would she make such basic mistakes?"

"Maybe she had a number she needed to remember—a number she didn't want anyone to find," Liza said slowly. "You remember what Detective Janacek asked us, Michael?"

He nodded. "He wanted to know if the room was just naturally messy, or if it could have been searched."

"Could somebody have tossed the place?" Buck's voice came over the speaker.

"I'm not sure," Liza admitted.

"But it could have been," Michael said more quickly. "And if so, it's a number the killer never got."

"What exactly are these numbers?" Michelle impatiently jumped ahead.

Liza consulted her copy. "Okay, two, three, five, three again, eight, one, nine, two, and five."

"Too long for a telephone number," Buck commented.

"Unless the last two numbers are an extension," Michael said. "It couldn't be in New York or L.A.—you have to start off with area codes."

Kevin nodded. "Where she took off and where she landed."

"The puzzle came from an in-flight magazine," Liza added. "Gemma had to write this down after she got on the plane."

"And she was met at the airport by a car that took her directly to Rancho Pacificano." Michael shrugged.

Over the speaker they heard the tickety-tack of computer keys being manipulated. "Just checking whether these could be ten-digit phone numbers with a number missing," Buck said. "But neither 235 nor, reading backward, 529 are valid area codes."

"Unless that's the part where the number was dropped. Are you sure you got all of them, Liza?" Michelle pressed.

Taking a deep breath, Liza looked hard at the scrap of paper in her hands. "The puzzle is symmetrical. That means I didn't mistake an answer for a clue . . ."

Michelle's annoyed sigh was loud enough to carry over the speaker phone. "In English, Liza."

"No. I don't think so."

"So what could it be?" Buck mused aloud. "Passcode, account number—"

That stirred a memory. "The resort here has safe-deposit boxes for the guests."

"Oh?" Michelle said.

Liza shrugged. "Unfortunately, Gemma didn't put anything in to be secured."

"And how did you find this out?" Michelle wanted to know.

"By overhearing," Liza answered. "Artie Kahn was at the front desk, making inquiries."

"Doing more work for Gemma now that she's dead than he ever did while she was alive." Michelle sniffed.

Liza paid no attention, looking at the somewhat scrunched puzzle in her hand. "I don't know if it makes a difference, but the first three numbers are all in the top third of the puzzle. The next four are in the second third, and they come in pairs. The last two are in the last two boxes of the puzzle, separated but near to one another."

Buck spoke after a moment of silence. "That would make . . . 235, 38, 19, and maybe 25."

"Well, there's a 235 almost under our noses," Michael said. "We're on the second floor of the building, aren't we?"

Mrs. Halvorsen spoke up. "Room 206."

"Suite 206, actually," Liza corrected as she got up, grabbed Michael's arm, and headed for the door. "Room 235 can't be that far away."

The main resort building was large and rambling, flinging off wings apparently at random.

Most likely to provide better views for the rooms, Liza thought.

They had a couple of wrong starts and some wandering along hallways before they finally came to Room 235. The door didn't look much different from the one to Liza's suite—or Gemma Vereker's for that matter.

Taking a deep breath, Liza raised her hand and knocked. No answer.

Liza forced her racing thoughts into some form of order. The room could be vacant, or the occupant could be out. This didn't necessarily mean they'd burst in on another dead body.

Still, that idea made her rap more forcefully when she tried knocking for a second time.

"Who's there?" a rather blurred voice asked, its tone sharp.

Liza stood with her mouth open for a second before answering, "Liza Kelly." It didn't quite have as much oomph as saying, "This is the police."

Still, the door rattled open to reveal Roy Conklin with a full case of bed head. "I started off resting my eyes and must have dropped off," he apologized, trying to pat his hair back into order. "What's up?"

She glanced over at Michael. What had seemed like a great inspiration now seemed a little silly. Still, she decided to go on. "Do the numbers three, eight, one, nine, two, and five mean anything to you?" she asked, wincing at how lame her voice sounded even in her own ears.

"They might be in pairs." Michael tried to help. "Three-eight, one-nine, two-five."

"Or maybe even thirty-eight, nineteen, and twenty-five?" Liza suggested.

The look on Roy's face incontrovertibly showed that he had no idea what the numbers might mean. His eyes, however, showed that he was wondering how to get help against a pair of apparent maniacs.

Liza quickly decided that explanations would not make either of those looks go away, so she decided to cut her losses. "Well," she said, "it was just a chance. Sorry we disturbed you. We'll get out of your hair now."

She could have kicked herself for that last line as Roy's hand went back to his disheveled hair.

They came down the side passage and almost reached the main hallway when Liza saw Charley Ormond rushing past with a camera crew. Catching hold of Michael's arm, she drew back.

"Three guesses where she's heading," Liza whispered.

"So where do we go?" Michael asked.

"If Mrs. H. answers the door, she'll send them here," Liza said. "Otherwise, they'll head for the elevator. Either way she'll catch up to us." She gazed down the hallway and then dragged Michael along with her to the fire stairs. Liza pushed the door open, pulled him through to the landing, then left the door slightly ajar.

A second later, she saw Roy Conklin padding into view in his stocking feet, still rumpled and carrying a plastic ice bucket. But he never made it to the ice machine.

Charley Ormond and her crew caught him in the middle of the hall. Roy froze like a deer caught in the camera spotlight as Charley shoved a mike in his face.

"Have you heard that Gemma Vereker has died?" she asked excitedly.

Poor Roy stood there with his lips curved in something like a smile. The last time Liza had seen a "natural" expression like that, it had been on the face of the guest of honor at a funeral—one that should have had a closed casket.

"That—that's terrible news," he said, still with that ghastly smile. "Are you sure?"

"We've gotten reports." Charley had her back to the

camera, and Liza could see the bafflement on the reporter's face as she tried to get something she could broadcast. "It's possible the whole tournament may be canceled."

"How terrible," Roy said again. "This tournament represents a very important juncture for sudoku, with the national coverage—"

"Yes, very important." Charley cut him off. "And it must be a great shock that such a famous star like Gemma, after devoting her time—"

"What?" Roy paused for a second, still with that awful rictus smile. Still worse, Liza saw nervous perspiration— "flop sweat" as actors called it—had begun pouring from his armpits, plastering his thin shirt till it clung like a second skin to his pudgy form. "Yes, very sad for a celebrity to die. Terrible."

The sweat stain actually met across his chest, making his nipples plainly visible.

"Yes." When Charley realized she was echoing along with him, she shook her head and quickly moved to end this disaster of an interview. "Thanks very much for your time, Professor Conklin."

"Yes, well, you're welcome." Roy still stood awkwardly, in front of the camera, shifting his ice bucket from hand to hand, still flashing that frozen grin.

Charley just ran her hand across her throat in a cutting gesture and led the crew off in silence. Roy padded back to his room, probably looking for a fresh shirt.

"Now I see why he prefers to take the back way," Liza whispered. "Poor guy."

"More like 'poor Charley,' " Michael replied. "After an interview like that, I wouldn't be surprised to catch her shoving a tumbleweed under Roy's bed tonight." He stuck his head out. "I think the coast is clear."

As they retraced the route to Liza's suite, he began to chuckle. "Maybe I can use that sweat bit in my script, with somebody being interrogated. Otherwise—well, that was entertaining, but not exactly useful."

"And you were a lot of help." Looking back on her own

stumbling conversation with Roy, Liza felt her face go red. "Why didn't you stop me before I left our suite?"

Michael shrugged. "It seemed a good idea at the time," he offered. "And sometimes those sideways jumps of logic you make seem to work."

"Yeah," Liza muttered, stomping along the plush carpeting. "Sometimes."

They came back to Suite 206 and announced their less than complete success. "We wound up at Roy Conklin's room," Liza said.

"It's at the end of a hall, well away from anyone," Michael added. "You've got to give the resort credit. That's probably exactly the way Roy likes it."

"He had no idea what those numbers meant, by the way, and was probably kind of annoyed at being woken up to be asked." Liza finished their report. "That's one idea gone like a busted balloon. I'm hoping someone else had an inspiration while we were away."

The discussion had continued in their absence. And like Michael, the four on the phone conference had tried treating the mystery numbers as pairs.

"Let's see." Kevin frowned in puzzlement. "Could it be some kind of measurement?"

"Huh," Buck replied. "Although 38–19–25 sounds kinda top-heavy—"

His musings were interrupted by an audible smack— obviously Michelle decided to apply her editorial comment directly to his shoulder.

"Reminds me of high school," Mrs. Halvorsen piped up.

Spinning toward Mrs. H., Liza stared at her, open-mouthed. A quick glance around showed Kevin and Michael doing the same.

Liza tried to remember what her neighbor looked like when she was younger. All she could recall was a petite, older lady. *Surely she couldn't . . .* Liza thought helplessly. *Or could she have had a high school friend that busty?*

Luckily, Liza didn't speak.

Mrs. H. continued on, cheerfully unaware of the consternation she'd just caused. "The school had just gotten them in when I started as a freshman. But I still remember the combination for my locker: thirty-eight right, seventeen left, and twenty-six right. It's very close, isn't it?"

"Uh . . . yeah," Kevin said, still a little slack-jawed.

"A combination." Buck's voice came slowly from the phone speaker. "Could be."

Michelle's response was considerably less pleased. "But for what?"

Liza shook her head. "Whatever it is, the number is apparently 235."

19

"All right," Buck Foreman said over the phone connection. "So where would we find lockers around this joint?"

"They must have some sort of health club here." Kevin put the idea forward.

"Right." Liza went for the writing desk in the sitting room. "Somewhere here we've got to have a guide to the amenities."

She found it, located the number for the Health and Fitness Facility, as it was called, and punched in the number on her cell phone.

The only problem was, the Health and Fitness Facility was a very select operation. They did have lockers, but they didn't run up as high as 235.

"Damn!" Liza said, breaking the connection. "What the hell else around here would have a lock on it as well as a number that goes up in the two hundreds?"

"It would also have to be something that Gemma would have noticed," Michelle added.

"So what would she have noticed?" Buck asked. "What were her interests?"

"Acting," Liza replied. "Sudoku."

"Drinking," Michael suggested with a laugh.

"You're not as funny as you think, Langley," Michelle rasped. "If the story you're telling is correct, that's why Gemma couldn't rouse herself when she began having distress."

"Uh—I guess you're right." Michael looked at his feet, abashed. "Sorry I spoke."

"No." Liza grabbed his arm. "Something you just said—it's stirring some sort of memory."

"About drinking?" Michael asked.

"Liza, this is in dubious taste," Michelle complained.

"Drinking," Liza repeated, "and animals."

"Could this have been about the bugs?" Mrs. H. piped up.

"I think—it was real animals," Liza said.

"After we found the bugs, Michael asked Kevin about the stables, because his room—"

"Right, right." Liza wrinkled her nose at the memory of the barnyard smell. "We were at the stables, wondering if the horses belonged to the resort or if guests boarded their own animals."

She suddenly whipped around to Kevin. "And then Kevin mentioned that people could board their own wine for use in the restaurant—"

The lightbulb went off over Kevin's head, and he joined his voice with Liza's. "In wine lockers!"

When they tried to place a call to Angus the chef, they merely got reception for Angus the restaurant. And if they weren't making reservations, the flunky there didn't want to talk to them, much less put them through to the boss.

In the end, Liza and Kevin went down to beard the chef in his kitchen, leaving Michael to keep talking with Buck and Michelle. Liza didn't quite like the idea of leaving Mrs. Halvorsen alone on the line with her sometime partner. Who knows what innocent comment might be elicited and stored up for ammunition?

Coming out of the elevator, Liza and Kevin nipped

across the lobby and took the back route to the event rooms. They picked an empty one, entered, and then Kevin led the way to the inconspicuous door that led to the kitchen.

Angus the chef wasn't the same gleaming figure in white from the haggis ceremony. He wore a more worka-day chef's outfit, and it was getting a little sweaty as he and his staff created the next round of meals.

The short, stocky chef obviously remembered Kevin from his foray to get ice and meat tenderizer for Liza's black eye. That didn't necessarily mean he was happy to see him again.

"Can't ye's see I'm a wee bit busy right now?" he de-manded as he mixed some sort of sauce over a high heat. The smell was delicious, although the look he gave the in-truders in his domain verged on poisonous.

"Ye'll have to see the maitre d' to arrange for that, and he'll not be in for a while yet." The chef now directed more of his attention to his saucepan than his guests.

"We don't want to get a wine locker," Liza said. "We just want to find out if one of the other guests has one."

"Well, can't ye ask them?" Angus went pale and fum-bled a little with his pot as the obvious thought hit him. "Or do ye mean one of . . . *those* guests?"

Liza nodded. "Maybe *had* would have been the better word."

Angus turned his sauce over to one of his assistants and led Liza and Kevin through the empty restaurant. The flunky at the reservations desk lost a lot of his hot and cold running attitude when the boss showed up. And although the maitre d' was the one who entered new applicants for the wine lockers, Mr. Flunky knew where the book was kept.

"Besides our regular guests, we have a number of local residents who'll leave a few special vintages with us for a good dinner," the young man babbled as he opened a large, leather-bound ledger.

"As many as two hundred and thirty?" Kevin asked in his best managerial voice.

Mr. Flunky flipped to the end of the book. "At this point, we have two hundred and thirty-seven."

"Who is Number 235?" Liza leaned forward, trying to read upside down as the young man ran his finger down a column.

"A Ms. G. Vereker of New York and Malibu . . ." The flunky's thin veneer of sophistication broke. "Gemma Vereker the actress—the woman who—"

"Yes, yes," Liza interrupted, patting the young man on the arm. "You might want to keep that under your hat for the time being." She sighed. "At least until the police start asking you questions."

"The police?" Kevin asked when they were safely alone in the elevator again. "Why do you—"

"For one thing, I'm not sure whether Angus—or Fergus Fleming, for that matter—would let us anywhere near that locker," Liza said. "Detective Janacek is the guy with the weight to leverage them. For another thing, I don't want anyone able to suggest that we could have monkeyed around with whatever might be in there."

"Well, if it's just a nice Riesling, I guess Angus could come up with something good to go with it," Kevin groused, "and to go with the egg on our faces."

But when Liza got back up to her suite, everyone else agreed with her. She got out her cell phone and contacted Pete Janacek.

The detective sounded frankly dubious when he heard about the sudoku clue. But he got quiet and listened when he heard about wine locker 235 being leased out to Gemma Vereker.

Janacek arrived armed with a search warrant and trailed by a very frustrated Oliver Roche.

Liza and her friends met them in the lobby.

"So where is this wine cellar?" the cop asked. He waved the warrant in one hand. The other held a sealed clear plastic envelope containing Gemma's original sudoku.

"It's downstairs under the kitchen." Roche was just about dancing around the police detective. "I'm sure you didn't have to go to the effort of securing a warrant. We could have arranged—"

Janacek shook his head. "If this turns out to be for real, I want this search to be completely legit."

They were able to bypass both Angus and the supercilious young man at the reservation desk. By now the restaurant's wine waiter had arrived, distinguished with a little flattened pan hanging round his neck on a chain.

Kevin couldn't resist pointing. "Do you actually use that?"

"No," the waiter replied, "but it impresses the hell out of people with more money than taste."

When Janacek showed him the warrant, the waiter escorted them downstairs. The restaurant's stock of wine rested in floor-to-ceiling racks spaced out across the dimly lit room. Three of the walls were covered with wooden cabinets bearing a variety of locks.

The waiter led them to one bearing a brass plate with an engraved 235—and a combination lock.

"And this belongs to Gemma Vereker?" Janacek asked.

"Strictly speaking, the contents do," the waiter replied. "I checked our wine book when I heard about all of this."

The detective looked from the lock to the puzzle in his other hand. "And you think these numbers down here are the combination?"

"We think it's worth a try," Liza said.

Shaking his head, Janacek began to twist the dial. At the final 25, the lock clicked open. The cop's eyebrows rose as he shot Liza an impressed look.

Roche made a little growling noise deep in his throat.

Removing the lock, Janacek opened the cabinet to reveal a racklike arrangement for bottles, but no wine. Instead, a thick manila envelope lay on the dark wood.

"Hold it," Janacek told the bystanders, who were all craning their necks for a better look. He directed them back, put away the puzzle, then took out a pair of latex gloves and an empty plastic envelope—a large one.

After donning the gloves, he gingerly picked up the envelope. "The return address is a bank up in L.A. And it's addressed to Gemma Vereker in New York."

Carefully removing the contents, the detective scanned the first page. "It's a letter from the branch manager, expressing some concern about the activity in the lady's accounts. Seems it's changed during her absence in New York."

He riffled through the rest of the pages. "These are just account records. They show money coming in and going out." Janacek stopped about halfway through, then moved quickly on to the end. "And from this point on, the money just seems to be going out—to somebody named Arthur Kahn."

20

"Arthur . . ." Liza blinked. "You mean Artie Kahn? He's Gemma Vereker's business manager."

Detective Janacek rattled the sheaf of papers in his hand. "From the looks of this, he's certainly been giving her the business."

"He can't be that stupid. Gemma would kill him." Liza clearly remembered Gemma's grim expression talking about the results of successful celebrity—never being able to trust anyone. That had to go back to her younger days when her parents had mismanaged her finances until she was almost broke. Gemma had never forgiven them—and she'd be pitiless if she discovered Artie doing the same.

Then she remembered other things, like Artie's almost cringing response when he caught up with her here at Rancho Pacificano. Gemma had been brusque—downright hostile, even—as she dismissed him with a mention of discussing business on Monday.

In fact, Artie hadn't even known Gemma was coming to town. He'd only found out because he'd been tapped to pay for Gemma's helicopter transport from LAX to John Wayne Airport.

Liza realized that Janacek was staring at her, obviously expecting more information. She related everything that had just gone through her head. "Artie must have been desperate when Gemma turned up so unexpectedly."

"Quick, too," Janacek grunted. "Ian Quirk was dead less than two hours after that reception."

"Well, Ian always got plenty of publicity for game playing with his allergies," Liza said. "And Artie certainly would know about Gemma's much less publicized allergy to tumbleweeds. All he'd have to do was Google sudoku and allergies and then buy the peanut candy."

"After that, he'd have more time to research and prepare for the other murders." The detective frowned in thought. "I guess the more difficult ones would take more time. He'd have to get some sort of shellfish broth to do in Mr. Terhune and trap bees to get the venom for Ms. Basset. I guess he was just lucky to find two more people with allergies."

"Maybe not," Liza said. "I've heard that the allergy rate has been soaring among people in the industrialized world."

Janacek shook his head. "Lucky us. It certainly made his attack on Gemma Vereker look as if it were just one among a string of serial murders."

"Except there were differences," Liza pointed out. "You asked about Gemma's suite being searched because of the mess. Artie must have done that, looking for whatever she had on his embezzlement." She took a deep breath. "You can also check with Fergus Fleming about his visit earlier, asking if Gemma had left any business papers in the resort's safe."

That brought Janacek's head up. "Where did you find out about that?" he demanded, then asked, "Did she?"

"I spotted Artie at the reception desk and overheard him," Liza admitted. "And no, Gemma didn't leave anything."

"Well, we've got motive and opportunity," Janacek said.

"And I bet we could find out something about the means, too," Liza added.

The detective shook his head, though. "It's all circumstantial. A good lawyer, like your friend Hunzinger, could argue it all away. We'd have to get Kahn to admit what he did. And how the hell are we going to get him to do that?"

Liza reached out a hand. "There may be a way."

Liza's suggestion won her a place in the police van, where technicians sat monitoring Janacek's young partner's voice as he spoke softly over the wire he was wearing.

"Are you receiving?" Holmes muttered for about the tenth time. That turned into whistling at the sound of footsteps clattering down the wine cellar stairs.

"You Kahn?" Holmes asked, his voice just perfect for a snotty waiter from an upscale restaurant—which is what he was dressed as.

"Yes." Artie Kahn's voice came from the speakers. "You called me?"

"Yeah, I did. Nice outfit, dude."

"It lets me get in and out of here without being noticed." Kahn tried to sound tough, but Liza could hear the nervousness in his voice, too.

"Sure, I think you'd want to do that." Holmes dropped his bantering tone. "So, you got the money?"

"I really don't know what this is all about." For all Artie's attempts to come across as puzzled, what really came across was terror.

"Yes you do, or you wouldn't have come down here." Holmes was very much in his bad-cop persona, or in this case, his bad bad-guy persona. "See those cabinets? Our guests can rent them to store their own wines to use in the restaurant upstairs. Gemma Vereker did that—I saw her name newly entered in our record book. And since she was dead, I figured I'd cut the lock off and maybe score a couple of expensive bottles of whatever. Instead, I found something even pricier."

"Which locker?" Artie demanded.

"That's what you're paying twenty grand for," Holmes shot back. "Have you got the money?"

"I got everything I could—fifteen thousand," Artie said.

"You think you're gonna freakin' bargain with me?" The young guy's voice took on an uglier edge.

"It's a Sunday afternoon! The banks are closed! This is all I could collect!" No way was Artie bargaining. He sounded desperate.

"Awright, awright, I guess it will have to do," Holmes grumbled. "It's Number 239."

Liza heard the sound of a cabinet door being yanked open, then a sharp intake of breath from Artie. The envelope resting in the locker came from the same bank, and Gemma's New York address had been printed on it. But inside was just a thick wad of blank pages.

"From the glance I got, it would be pretty bad for you if this fell into the hands of the cops," Holmes said. "Aren't you lucky it got found by a reasonable businessman like me? I'll leave you to it—"

She heard sudden rushing steps, then Holmes saying, "What are you doing with that bottle?"

"Making sure you stay quiet," Artie Kahn said with all the viciousness of a trapped rat.

At the sounds of a scuffle, one of the techs leaned into a microphone, shouting, "Backup!"

An instant later, Liza heard Detective Janacek's voice. "Put it down, Mr. Kahn. This is the police. The detective you were just about to brain is wearing a wire."

When Janacek brought the handcuffed prisoner upstairs for questioning, Liza almost burst out, "That isn't Artie Kahn!"

At first she really didn't recognize the tall, thin, bald man in custody. With his Rancho Pacificano staff uniform, he could have been doing any job at the resort.

Then she looked harder, mentally adding Artie Kahn's customary fright wig and heavy-framed glasses. Yes, this was Gemma's manager. But without those props, he'd hardly rate a second glance.

Just as he said—he hadn't been noticed by anyone while killing all those people, Liza thought.

Artie's eyes darted around all over the place as he tried to cling to some shred of innocence. "Detective, I only tried to subdue that young man. He was trying to blackmail me—"

"No, you were trying to shut me up," young Holmes interrupted. "We've got you on tape."

"And while you might have had some trouble getting into banks on Sunday, we didn't," Janacek joined in. "You were pretty heavily invested when this latest financial bubble burst, and you've been using your client's funds to try and bail yourself out."

"Except you were losing that money, too," Holmes said, adding salt to the wound.

"If Gemma Vereker ever called you on it—especially given her history of management and financial foolishness—you wouldn't just face financial ruin, but prison." Janacek's voice was grim.

Kahn's eyes fastened on the detective now, his oh-so-ordinary face growing pale.

"Then there's this odd piece of floral décor you purchased for your office last year." Janacek gave Artie a knowing smile, but Liza knew this was the result of Buck Foreman's computerized sleuthing. "I can't quite believe where it was ordered from—a farm in Kansas specializing in tumbleweeds. But they have the records of sending you a dried tumbleweed—and we have the story about how your client made you put it away because she was allergic. Whatever happened to that plant, Artie? I suspect our lab people will find something on the tumbleweed under Ms. Vereker's bed that will trace back to you."

"Yeah," Holmes gibed. "Plant DNA, maybe."

"Or maybe just dust from your office basement." Janacek

was back to playing the calm, unflappable cop. "We've got you every step of the way for Gemma Vereker's murder, Artie. And it's just a matter of time until we start connecting you to the other three."

Artie's stooped shoulders had sagged a bit more with every fact the cops had hit him with. Then he suddenly jerked back, staring around again. "But I—you think . . ." He rose to his full height. "I want my lawyer."

Back upstairs as Liza recounted the story of the arrest to her friends, Michael shook his head. "Kahn should have cracked," he complained. "Caught by surprise, faced with a recording, seeing he had no way out . . . this was the psychological moment—he should have confessed everything."

"The psychological moment for a movie script, maybe," Kevin jeered. "That's not necessarily true in real life."

Liza sighed. No sooner was the crisis over than the men in her life started sniping at each other.

"As it happens, I know a lot about scripts *and* real life," Michael flared back. He obviously had a lot more to say, except he was interrupted by the bleat of his cell phone.

"Michael Langley here. Sid! What's up?" His face showed surprise, then horror. "You've got to be kidding me! So are they—what? They did *what*? Oh, please say you're kidding me, Sid."

His expression now reached all the way down to disgust. "So what do they want now?" Michael's eyebrows shot up. "When? How can I—well, maybe the first three scenes. Yeah, I guess I'll *have* to get started right away."

Shaking his head, he turned to the others. "The lead for *The Surreal Killer* attempted to bust out of rehab this morning by jumping into a tree from his room. Unfortunately, he landed on his head—and in the hospital."

"Are they canceling the project?" Liza asked with concern. She knew if that happened, the film might never get back on track again.

"No, the producer had the brainwave of casting a new

lead. No better actor than the first choice—except she's female." Michael rolled his eyes. "Of course, that means a complete rewrite."

"And they want it when?" she asked.

"Tomorrow," he sighed. "I'll have to come up with a few revised scenes to keep them off my back. Guess that's life."

"And film scripts," Kevin cackled, but Michael wasn't up for a fight anymore. He just leaned over and kissed Liza good-bye. "Gotta collect my stuff from the motel and head for the homestead. Take it easy," he said to Kevin. "And it was great to see you again, Mrs. H."

"Good-bye, Michael," she said.

"Maybe you could get your hazmat suit into the first scene," Liza suggested. "Then the killer opens it up to reveal—"

"Neat idea!" Michael turned back to kiss her again. "Thanks."

Kevin stared after Michael's retreating back with pure jealousy in his eyes. "You never do that with me."

"I don't tend to come up with useful ideas for running an inn," she pointed out. "Maybe that's because I spent too many years involved with the movies."

Mrs. Halvorsen's eyes went from Liza's to Kevin's and back again. "I can mention something useful," she said. "How about lunch?"

Liza put her hand to her stomach. There had been too much excitement for her to notice the empty feeling. But it came on pretty strong when Mrs. H. mentioned a meal.

"You've got to keep your strength up," the older woman went on. "Why don't the two of you go and get a bite? I couldn't eat a thing myself after all this. Maybe I'll take a nap and then catch a snack."

Now Liza shot her neighbor a sharp look. First and foremost, Elise Halvorsen was a matchmaker. No sooner was Michael out of the picture than Mrs. H. came up with a way to fix Liza up with Kevin.

"I don't know about you," Kevin said, "but I'm starving."

"Let's see if we can take the back way into the kitchen," Liza suggested. "I don't want to end up dealing with crowds."

Or any of the camera crews that should be arriving by now, she thought.

They never made it to the kitchen. Oliver Roche intercepted them in the hallway. "Ms. Kelly," he said, "I guess you're to be congratulated."

"Well, thank you," she replied hesitantly.

"I wonder if you could spare me a couple of minutes." The security man opened the door to one of the event rooms—one of the ones no longer in use for the competition as the number of contestants dwindled.

The place still remained set up for the tournament, though. As they entered, a figure rose from behind the timer's desk. Roy Conklin looked a little embarrassed with half a sandwich in his hand and a paper plate in front of him. "I—I didn't think anyone would be coming in here." He gestured to his plate. "It's nice to avoid the mob scene, and I like spending some quiet time in the same sort of place where we'll be competing in the final round."

He shifted away from his seat. "I'll gladly leave if you'd prefer."

"Not at all," Roche said with a phony joviality that set Liza's teeth on edge. He brought Liza and Kevin to the first row of tables, gestured for them to sit down, and then turned to Roy. "You're just the man I was hoping to find. Maybe you can help us thrash out the answer to all the murders here."

Roy blinked in confusion. "I thought I heard that the police had made an arrest."

"Oh, no." Roche shook his head. "That fellow was only responsible for the last one. We've got to zero in on who committed the other three."

He rested his hip against Roy's table and stared at Liza. "You were very clever with your little puzzle, using it to tie up that Hollywood jackass. From the looks of it, the police have him dead to rights."

"And I expect they'll get him on the others," Kevin said.

"No they won't," Roche told him flatly. "It's easy to think that the guy committed all those murders to set up the killing that was really important to him. But when you look at it, it's the other way around. This Kahn clown took advantage of the other murders to slip in an extra—one that would take him off the hook for fraud and whatever."

"And what leads you to believe that?" Liza had to ask.

"The guy turned out to be a complete basket case. He couldn't even figure out how to deal with that kid of Jan-acek's apparently blackmailing him." Roche flung out an angry hand. "Trying to belt him with a wine bottle! And what in hell was he going to do with the bottle—not to mention the body—after that?"

He shook his head scornfully. "No, Kahn was just a desperate shlub taking a lucky stab. The real murderer showed cleverness, even wit—and a kind of cold-blooded willingness to kill colleagues."

Liza jumped up from her seat. "That's it, Roche. I've heard—".

Roche slipped a pistol from under his jacket. "No, you haven't heard enough. We didn't even get to the big problem yet—motive. Why would someone go on a sudden killing spree? Although calling it a 'spree' makes it sound like too much fun. Because the killer had a very serious reason, an out-of-the-ordinary reason for getting rid of those sudoku people. Because I think the killer is also a bit of a nut."

Speaking of nuts, this guy is about to wave his gun around and accuse me of murder, Liza thought, looking into Roche's blazing eyes.

Kevin sat where he was, staring in disbelief—but following the gun. "Don't do anything stupid," he warned Roche.

The security man sneered right back at him. "Stupid? The stupid thing is believing your stupid theory—because the last murder had an obvious motive, one guy must have done them all. Bull! We all know who the murderer is—"

As Roche started to rage, Roy Conklin rose from his seat, grabbed the chair beside him, and smashed it down on the man's bald, red head.

Roche gave a groan and sprawled on his side.

"Roy! Thank God!" Liza said.

Then Roy scooped up Roche's pistol and trained it on Liza and Kevin. "Shut up and keep your hands where I can see them."

21

"Wha—what?" Liza's jaw didn't seem to be working right as she stared at the mousy academic holding the ex-cop's pistol. It was like one of those puzzle pictures—"What Does Not Belong Here?"

"Oh, don't look so surprised, Liza." Conklin trembled with anger as he glared at her. "You were in on it, weren't you? But I moved before your security friend here could turn his gun around and accuse me."

Roy bumped the table as he went to swing across it, sending Roche's unconscious form toppling to the floor. Conklin glanced down, almost showing regret. "He was just some worker bee trying to do his job."

Good thing Roche is past hearing that, Liza couldn't help thinking. *He'd have a fit.*

"But *you!*" Conklin poked his gun at her, looking really aggrieved. "That's your thing, isn't it? She solves sudoku puzzles—she solves mysteries." His voice dripped scorn—and his lips dribbled a little, too.

Well, Roche was right about one thing, Liza thought. *We're definitely dealing with a nut.*

"Roy, why . . ." she said aloud, and then stopped. Unbidden, the memory of his horrible, stilted performance in front of the cameras rose up—and also his breakfast conversation with Gemma Vereker. Liza remembered the pain in the professor's eyes as he talked about trying to promote sudoku. Obviously, he couldn't do that. And the people who did had to become an eccentric, a huckster, a diva, or a clown.

The clown was poor Scottie, Liza thought. *Babs was definitely a diva—so was Ian Quirk, although he might also go down as an eccentric. As for huckster, that might be an unkind way of looking at Will Singleton.* She drew a sharp breath. *Or me.*

So Roy Conklin had decided to clean out the money changers from the temple of sudoku, doubtless from the purest of motives. Or was there a less noble basis for his actions—like really corrosive jealousy?

"I tried to do some outreach, teaching that class on solving techniques," Conklin went on. "And out of all the people here for the tournament, nobody cared—until a *celebrity* did."

"She tried to do you a good turn, publicizing the class," Liza said.

"Patronizing me is more like it—the way she did when she told me how to become a celebrity."

"Well, you're sure to become a celebrity now, after killing three people," Kevin quipped.

Liza wished he would keep his mouth shut. If pushed, Roy might just decide to cover his trail by killing three more—Roche, Kevin, and Liza.

Instead, Conklin's mind was on escape. "I'll feel better once I put an international border between myself and the law." He nodded at Kevin. "You came here in a fancy sports car. We're going to use that to go to Mexico."

"What? But—"

Conklin waved away Kevin's attempted protests with his gun. "Shut up. We're going now—and we'll head out through the kitchen. I want to be well gone before this guy wakes up."

Reaching into the satchel beside him, he pulled out a Rancho Pacificano staff jacket and donned it single-handed. It was almost a perfect match with the nondescript pants he wore. Well, Artie Kahn had already shown how the resort's staff people were pretty much invisible. And come to think of it, Kevin had shown how easily those staff outfits were available.

Slowly, she rose from her seat. Kevin had served as a Special Forces type in the Army. She'd seen him use some unarmed combat moves. Maybe he could—

Conklin killed that idea as dead as Quirk, Babs, and Scottie. "You go first," he told Kevin. "Liza will be right with me. If you try anything funny, she gets it."

From the look on Kevin's face, he wasn't about to try anything.

They moved through the kitchen without anyone commenting on it. Roy came last with the pistol in his jacket pocket poking Liza in the spine. When they exited through a back door, Conklin nodded toward the parking structure in the distance. "I can see your car from here. Go get it. Liza will stay with me. Do I have to repeat myself about doing anything?"

Kevin silently went and drove up in the car a moment later.

"Leave the keys in, come out, and sit on the ground," Roy ordered. Then he grabbed Liza by the arm, keeping the gun to her head. "I'm getting in the back, and you're getting behind the wheel."

Once they were settled in with the pistol behind Liza's ear, Roy called for Kevin to get in the passenger's seat.

Then he told Liza, "Start the car and head south."

Soon enough, they were on a freeway heading for the border.

Liza found herself with more time to think.

He's micromanaging every step of the way rather than thinking long term, she realized. *That won't be good if things stop going his way.*

The little details were something Roy could control,

just as he'd meticulously laid out his plans to do in the sudoku celebrities. But it didn't look as if he'd put much
thought into an escape plan, something that would certainly involve uprooting his life. What could he expect to
do in Mexico? For that matter, how much money was he
carrying right now? As if reading her mind, Roy said, "It's
a shame we had to leave. I could have used that prize
money."

Yeah, especially since you killed the odds-on favorite,
Liza thought.

She tried to sneak a glance at her watch. Oliver Roche
wasn't going to stay unconscious forever. Roy hadn't even
attempted to tie him up or hide him. Suppose some staff
people came in to clean the room? Once Roche was found,
the clock would really start ticking.

At least the traffic was on the light side as they got on
the entrance ramp for the freeway. Roy glanced around.
"We should be in Mexico within three hours," he said.

Unless the cops try to stop us well before that. Liza
grimaced to herself. *And what will our geek with a gun do
then?*

She had an irreverent vision of Roy Conklin standing in
for Jimmy Cagney in the old movie, waving his pistol and
yelling, "Top of the world, Ma!"

More likely, there'd be some other tragedy—and she
and Kevin were under Conklin's gun.

"Know what I think?" she exclaimed. "I bet we can get
there in half that time!"

Matching her words, she pressed down on the gas pedal.
The Porsche leapt forward as if someone had goosed the
car, roaring down the ramp and swerving wildly into the
stream of traffic.

Liza remembered what had happened when she and
Kevin had driven off into the hills. And sure enough, as
their acceleration increased, the rear of the car began to
develop a mind of its own.

The faster they went, the scarier that shimmy became.
Liza could feel her body pressing against her seat belt with

every lurch. In the rear, Roy struggled to keep from being flung around. His left hand hung on to the top of Liza's seat with a death grip, while the pistol in his other hand kept poking into Liza's head with painful force.

"Stop!" Roy yelled. "Stop it now!"

"What are you gonna do?" Liza inquired, clinging to the wheel as best she could while flooring the gas. "Shoot me, and the car probably flies across the median. None of us survive."

Roy rose up, bracing himself in the cramped backseat. "I don't have to shoot you." His voice rose in a maniacal shriek. "I can shoot your boyfriend!"

To do that, though, he had to take the gun away from Liza's head.

As soon as Roy did that and before he could aim at Kevin, Liza hit the brakes.

Tires shrieked, the nose of the Porsche seemed to dive, and the momentum pitched Liza and Kevin against the shoulder straps of their seat belts with bruising force.

As for Roy, who wasn't strapped in, the force of the stop launched him into the air. He had a short flight, though. It came to a thumping end against the Porsche's windshield.

Liza had feared that Roy might actually smash through the reinforced glass. The stuff didn't even crack, though she couldn't be sure about his skull. The impact didn't do a lot for his baby face, either. Roy bounced off, hard, and lay stunned across the console.

Kevin made a lunge for the gun, disarming Conklin. Liza allowed herself to sag over the wheel, ignoring honking horns, various fingers, and even the growing wail of oncoming police sirens.

In the end, the cops contented themselves with issuing a stern warning to Liza over the unorthodox method she'd used to subdue her kidnapper. Conklin was rushed off to a hospital, where he was found to have no problems— medically, at least. Three counts of premeditated murder would probably leave him with a lot of prison time to spend perfecting his sudoku technique.

Oliver Roche also emerged from the hospital, his head swathed in bandages, trumpeting that his investigation had actually solved the case. He would have sounded a lot more convincing if he hadn't had to explain the bit about turning his back on the murderer to get his head cracked and his gun stolen. Needless to say, Roche never heard about being reinstated as a cop. Judging from the look on Fergus Fleming's face while he watched some of the carrying on, Roche was on borrowed time at Rancho Pacificano.

When Will Singleton caught up with Liza, his expression blended relief with disappointment. "You know, you and Conklin were almost in a dead heat for first place throughout the tournament," he told her. "But when neither of you showed up for the Winner Takes All round—"

"So who did win?" Liza asked.

"Doc Dunphy, as he likes to be called now." Liza caught a hint of a grin under Will's facial foliage. "When she interviewed him, Charley Ormond seemed quite taken. I may have created my own worst competition."

"After his experiences, I think old Doc will be a bit more wary of the whole celebrity thing," Liza said. "Let the new king enjoy his crown."

"But you . . ." Will broke off when Liza made a face and waved off his apologies.

"There's always next year," she told him.

Ava Barnes called, demanding an exclusive for the *Oregon Daily*. Liza agreed to a twenty-minute interview.

Charley Ormond hoped for a SINN exclusive, too, but Liza let Will do the talking.

A frantic Michael showed up at the police station. He was lucky no cops had caught him on his high-speed progress from Westwood to Newport Beach.

"What about your script?" Liza asked.

"The hell with that," he answered. "I had to make sure you were all right."

Once he was assured of that, Michael immediately started in on Kevin for letting Liza get into danger. Kevin was already in a bad mood. The police had discovered the reason for the Porsche's erratic behavior at high speed. Kevin hadn't replaced the gas cap correctly after filling up the car, and fuel had been escaping to get onto the rear wheels. Wounded right in his masculinity, Kevin was restrained from hauling off and belting Michael only by some severe words by Mrs. H.

In the end, she sent them both out the door of the suite. Liza had distanced herself from the whole scene by going out onto the balcony. Evening was coming on, and she was enjoying the view of the bay getting darker while the lights of the surrounding town began to sparkle.

"Restful," Mrs. Halvorsen said as she joined Liza outside.

"Which is more than we can say for the rest of this weekend." Liza shook her head. "We have to fly back home tomorrow, just when I feel that I could really use some pampering."

"Maybe you could take some more time off," Mrs. H. suggested. "Go to the Killamook Inn for a couple of days."

"Yeah, well . . . the days might not be a problem, but the nights up there with Kevin—not such a good idea."

Mrs. H. sighed with the disappointment of the dedicated matchmaker. "When you were a little more than a toddler, I managed to get a good deal on a kiddie pool."

"I remember that!" Liza said. "On hot afternoons I'd come over, you'd fill it with a hose, and I would splash."

Mrs. Halvorsen nodded with a reminiscent smile. "For the next year, you used to call me Mrs. Pool. You know, I think I still have it somewhere in my garage."

Liza chuckled. "Great! Maybe we can dig it out. I'll set it up in my backyard and sit out in it—probably with Rusty in my lap—and try to do sudoku."

"That's the spirit!" Mrs. Halvorsen joined in the laughter.

"It might not be too bad, especially the sudoku." Liza

got a bit more serious. "Just one other thing. I'll need a
beach umbrella, big enough to shade the whole pool."

"Why ever would you need that?" Mrs. H. wanted to
know.

"It's going to be a long time before I'll feel comfortable
with tanning goo," Liza told her. "A very long time."

Sudo-cues

Dot's an Idea

Written by Oregon's own leading sudoku columnist, Liza K

We've talked in the past about sudoku size in terms of the number of initial clues. This time around, I'm concerned with the physical size of the puzzle. Back in the start-up days of this column, working with a single newspaper, I had some animated discussions with the layout people, warning that about three inches square was the smallest they could get away with shrinking a sudoku. And that's scarcely ideal.

Unlike crossword blanks, which just need to be large enough to take a letter, an empty sudoku square has to act as a workspace, a place to list the possible candidates that could occupy that position in the puzzle. In a perfect universe, such a space should be a half-inch or three-quarters of an inch square, but that would mean four-and-a-half or seven-inch sudoku. In a world where newsprint is expensive and comic strip panels have shrunk to postage-stamp size, newspapers just aren't going to do that.

Unless the periodical is devoted to sudoku, the most generous allotment of space is about three inches, meaning a blank space takes up a little more than one-third of a square inch. I've seen some puzzles reduced to two inches square. How are you supposed to fit all the necessary candidates in there? Using the sharpest pencil, you're reduced to using a letter size usually reserved for really objectionable clauses in contracts.

I tend to use the margins around the puzzles to list the missing numbers in columns, rows, and subgrids. And like a lot of citizens of Sudoku Nation who aren't twenty-nine anymore, I've used photocopiers to enlarge teeny-tiny sudoku to more manageable working proportions. That works fine if you're in a home office or a business not patrolled by the Photocopy Police. But suppose you're riding (not driving!) to work and you've got to work with a puzzle as it is?

Even if you manage to fit in the candidates, you're expected to erase them as they're eliminated. More likely you'll erase several that you need trying to get rid of the one you don't. And given the state of newsprint, you'll end up with a grayish smear—or at worst, a hole.

Recently, I've noticed some people using a simpler method on these miniature puzzles, a positional notation to mark possible candidates.

That's a very fancy way of saying they use dots instead of numbers. Let's zoom in on a rare phenomenon, a sudoku blank with a full range of candidates. Listing them would probably look like this:

$$
\begin{array}{ccc}
1 & 2 & 3 \\
4 & 5 & 6 \\
7 & 8 & 9
\end{array}
$$

Not easy to do in under a quarter inch of space. But it takes a lot less pencil work (and space) to represent these same positions with dots:

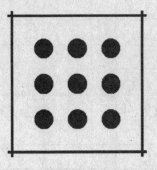

Instead of erasing, you just cross out eliminated candidates, like so:

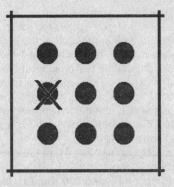

Let's take the system for a test-drive with a fairly simple puzzle.

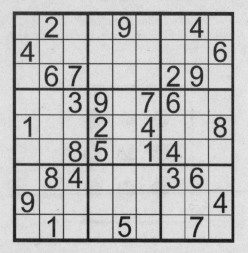

This won't take you more than halfway down the list of twelve standard sudoku solving techniques. There are no X-wings, no swordfish, no need for the more esoteric forms of logic chains, and if you're halfway decent at sudoku solving, no need to look in the back of the book.

So, let's start with the first technique—hidden singles. Looking across the middle tier of subgrids, starting down from Row 4, you can find the number 8 in both the left-hand set of nine spaces and in the right-hand box. The center subgrid has only three open spaces. With the 8s in Row 5 and Row 6 prohibiting two of those spaces, we can place an 8 as shown in Row 4.

That center tier also has two 4s, in the central box and the right-hand box, respectively. Crosshatching with the two 4s in the upper-left-hand and lower-right-hand boxes leaves only one space in the leftmost box in the center tier. We've placed a 4 in there, as shown.

The bottom tier of three subgrids also has two boxes

with a 4. From their locations, they eliminate six of the eight available blank spaces in the bottom center box. A 4 in the central box in the tier above eliminates another possible space, leaving only one, where we have marked another 4.

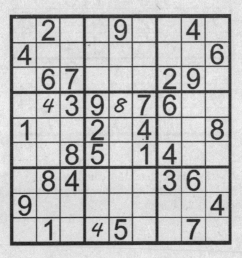

So now we have thirty clues and three solved spaces—forty-eight spaces to go.

At this point in the puzzle there are no naked singles. Usually, you'd try this technique on the more filled-in rows, columns, or boxes. The central box has seven spaces filled, but more than one possibility for the remaining two. Row 4 has three blank spaces, but each of those has more than one possible occupant.

Our usual next step is to start nominating candidates. Here's what the puzzle would look like if you used the usual method of filling empty spaces with small numbers:

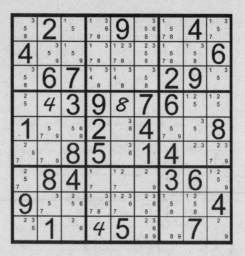

That yields more than 150 candidates, if you're into counting. From here on, the techniques are aimed at reducing that number, bit by bit.

Here's what the puzzle would look like in dot notation:

The first of these reducing acts is row and box/column and box interactions. The idea here is not to focus on a single space but to see whether segments of rows or columns as broken up by the puzzle subgrids can possibly hold a given number. Then we can eliminate that candidate from other segments of a column or row.

For instance, look at the vertical string of boxes in the left side of the puzzle. The top box contains a 2 right at the top of Column 2, thus eliminating 2s from the segments of Column 1 and Column 3 up there. Moving down to the middle box, Column 3 has two clues in its central segment, and the remaining open space stands right next to a 2 in Row 4. That means that the value 2 can only be found in the segment from Column 1 (we've starred the dots representing the possible placements). By process of elimination, 2 can only appear in Column 3 in the bottom left box in the string. Again, we've starred the two possible candidates. The net result is two dots Xed out at the bottom of Column 1.

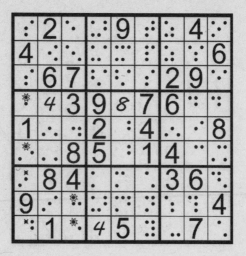

Next, let's look for naked pairs, where a row, column, or box shares a pair of spaces with two and only two identical candidates.

One just about leaps out at you from the center box—the two remaining open spaces contain dots representing only 3 and 6. Looking up and down Row 5, that eliminates four more candidates.

How about hidden pairs? Like the naked variety, these are twosomes that can only be found in a couple of spaces in a column, row, or box. Unfortunately, they conceal themselves among several other candidates in those spaces. You can see one in the center right box. Check the intersection of Row 5 and Column 7 and see the dots for 7 and 9 alongside the dot for 5. Then look at Row 6: Column 9 has the same 7 and 9 dots in the 2379. You can eliminate three excess candidates.

	2			9			4	
4								6
	6	7				2	9	
	4	3	9	8	7	6		
1			2		4			8
		8	5		1	4		
	8	4				3	6	
9								4
	1		4	5			7	

Clumps of candidates can come in larger sizes, maybe even as quintuplets and sextuplets. As a matter of practicality, sudoku solvers rarely search higher than naked or hidden triples. And if you look in the bottom center box, you can find three spaces that represent the only places with shared dots representing 3, 6, and 8. This may be a little difficult—you have to train yourself to ignore eliminated dots while scanning for valid candidates. Bringing the hidden 3, 6, and 8 dots into the open involves Xing out the dots representing five other candidates.

That, fellow solvers, takes us through the first six techniques. Now we start up again. Having eliminated some candidates, it might pay off to scan along the boxes, rows, and columns to see if we may have created any single candidates. And here's one in Column 6 at the intersection with Row 7—there's only one dot in the 9 position left, which we've starred, putting an X over the dot representing 2. Then, moving up the column to the intersection with Row 2, we find the only remaining 2 in that particular column. We've starred that one, too, Xing out the remaining dots.

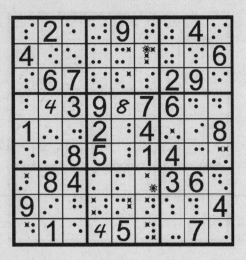

So here's the puzzle filled out with all the sure numbers.

At this point we've only added six answers to the original thirty clue spaces, but after searching out a couple more hidden pairs, you'll eliminate enough additional candidates to start a logical chain reaction among the remaining forty-five unknowns.

So here at least is a taste of using positional notation. I purposely kept the sample puzzle simple, because I believe there's a bit of a learning curve involved. I managed to work all of the less complicated techniques using dots, but I'll admit that without numbers to fasten on, I had a harder time spotting the hidden triple, much less trying to hunt up X-wings and swordfish. As is the case in most things sudoku, it involves educating the eyes to spot something different.

The dots offer a workable alternative for small-scale puzzles, but they require practice. It's certainly worth learning if you do a lot of on-the-go sudoku.

If you have fun with it, that's great. Otherwise, well, there's the trusty copy machine.

Puzzle Solutions

Puzzle from page 30

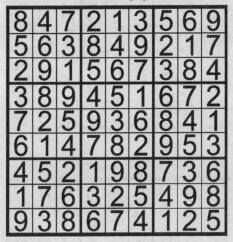

Puzzle from page 95

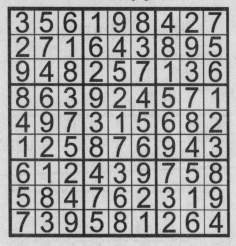

Puzzle from page 98

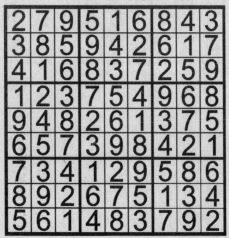

Puzzle from page 137

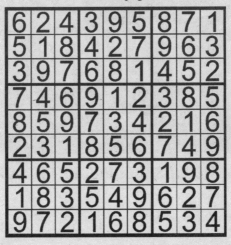

Puzzle from page 212

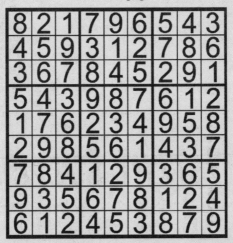